JACK KNIFED

A Detective Jack Stratton Novel

Christopher Greyson

Greyson Media

JACK KNIFED

Copyright: Christopher Greyson
Published: December 10th 2015

Find out more about the author and upcoming books online at www.ChristopherGreyson.com

Table of Contents

CHAPTER 1

A Fork In The Head

Six-year-old Jack Stratton sat at his kitchen table and ate his standard dinner: milk and cereal. As his big, brown eyes scanned the maze game on the back of the cereal box, he used his finger to trace the route Tony the Tiger needed to go to find his way home.

At the end of the hallway of his rundown apartment, his mom's bedroom door creaked open. Jack's head rose as he looked with anticipation, but it wasn't her; it was the creepy guy who had started to live with them a week ago. The guy lumbered out and scratched at his fat belly that hung below a dirty white tank top. The jerk—as Jack called him—strutted around as if he owned the place.

Jack swallowed and kept his head down, trying to focus on Tony the Tiger's face. He liked Tony. Tall and strong, he was always smiling and giving a big thumbs-up. He was what Jack imagined a dad would be like.

"What the hell is this?" the guy snapped.

Jack slid the cereal box to the side and glanced at the milk spots on the table. "I think I spilled some milk," he admitted.

"You just left it like that?" As the guy's arms flung wide, his big belly bounced. "You think I want to live like a pig?"

Confused, Jack scanned the old, rundown kitchen; it had crap everywhere. His mom was never much for keeping things clean.

Jack was a tough little kid; adults rarely intimidated him. Growing up in a whorehouse, you learned to be hard, because soft wasn't an option. He ignored the guy's rant and went back to his cereal box.

The guy stepped closer and stood over him. "Did you hear me?"

When Jack didn't answer, the guy smacked Jack across the side of the head. Half-chewed cereal flew out of his mouth, all over Tony the Tiger. Jack started to run, but the guy grabbed him by the back of the shirt and threw him to the ground.

"Punk." He shoved the chair out of the way. "I'll teach you some manners." He took two strides and pushed Jack into the corner of the kitchen and beat him.

"STOP!" Jack's little voice screamed.

The guy reared back his hand and balled it into a fist. Each blow hurt like hell. Jack's tiny arms tried to shield his stomach as the guy slammed his fist into his ribs. Jack struggled to use his legs to kick the jerk off, but it was like a toothpick smashing against a stone wall.

Suddenly, Jack heard his mother's voice cry out, "Don't touch my son!"

He grunted, reached back and shoved her into the wall.

Jack closed his eyes and gritted his teeth as he waited for the next blow to come—but it never did. Instead, he heard a strange "thunk." Then the guy stumbled back and shrieked like a banshee.

Slowly, Jack opened one eye and looked up to see the oddest sight. The guy stood screaming in the middle of the kitchen, with a fork stuck in his head.

"Get the hell out of my house," his mother yelled. She threw anything she could get her hands on.

As objects were hurled, the guy screamed and ran around in a circle with the fork still wobbling on top of his head. It looked so weird, Jack forgot about the beating he'd just taken and laughed. After a minute of being repeatedly pelted—and one direct hit in the face with a glass saltshaker—the man fled out the front door. Jack's mother grabbed the jerk's jacket and chucked it into the hallway. "Get lost, loser." She slammed the door shut.

When she turned back around, she looked at Jack with wide eyes. "Are you okay?"

He lifted himself up to a sitting position and nodded.

His mom walked over and knelt. She reached out and stroked the side of his face. "Are you sure you're okay?"

Jack nodded rapidly.

She helped him get up. She glanced at the cereal that had been dumped in the chaos. "Do you want me to make you some dinner?"

He looked up at her and smiled; she hadn't made him dinner in months. As she opened the cabinets, her faint smile vanished—every cabinet was empty. She shut the last one, and stared at him for a minute. Jack shifted uncomfortably. Her head snapped up. She turned and went to the high cabinet above the refrigerator. She pushed some pots around and then pulled out a dark navy box. Her blue eyes sparkled. "What about some mac and cheese?"

"Yeah. That sounds great, Mommy."

Jack ran to get the bowls while she filled a pot with water. He came over and stood beside her while they waited for it to boil.

She glanced at his swollen cheek; her shoulders slumped, and her lip trembled. Jack thought she was about to cry; he'd never seen her do that. She turned away and dumped the hard, dry pasta into the pot. Gently, he reached out and touched her arm. She looked back at him and smiled.

As the little cloud of steam from the boiling water rose, Jack got lost looking into the fog…

"Jack?"

He opened his eyes to see the fog rising high inside the shower.

"Jack?" Replacement called out again, as she knocked on the bathroom door. Her voice snapped him back to reality.

"Hold on." He turned off the water and headed for the sink.

Jack stared at the bathroom mirror, still fogged up from his shower. He reached out and cleared a small circle. His dark-brown eyes were the same, but it wasn't a little boy who stared back at him anymore; it was the face of a twenty-six-year-old man. The nightmares that had been keeping him up all night had begun to fill his head during the day, too.

Jack shaved close, but felt he needed a haircut badly. His deep-brown eyes had small semicircles underneath; he hadn't been sleeping well because of the nightmares he kept having about his childhood.

He pushed back his dark-brown hair and rolled his broad shoulders. Most of the time when he looked in the mirror he saw a handsome guy, but not today. Right now, he almost scared himself. Jack rinsed his mouth out and glared back at his reflection one more time.

"Jack?" Replacement knocked again.

He rolled his eyes.

Is she ever gonna take no for an answer?

"Yeah." He opened the bathroom door and walked past her. Grabbing his jacket, he headed for the front door.

"Please?" She jumped in front of him and clasped her hands together.

"No," he said sternly. "I don't want you along. Not on this." Jack walked around her and opened the front door. She slipped under his arm and out in front of him. He had to stop short. Replacement's five-foot-four petite frame stood square in the middle of the hallway as she blocked the way.

He fought back a grin. "You look about as threatening as a puppy," he joked. He knew she could hold her own. She'd shown that in spades last month on their last adventure.

"Please?" Dressed in a T-shirt, blue jeans, and little fur-trimmed brown boots that matched her brunette ponytail, she smiled up at him. The outfit gave her a bit of a country look. She was a fit and attractive nineteen-year-old.

He exhaled. He looked down at her pouting face and those damn cute little dimples that melted his heart, and answered, "No." He pulled the door closed and walked around her. As he stomped down the small hallway, the thin carpet did little to dampen the heavy pounding of his heels.

"Please? I'll be good. Please?" She raced after him.

"How many times do I have to say no? I don't want to go. Why would I want you to be there?"

Jack rushed down the stairs. The railing shook as he thundered past. The old door swung open with a creak, and he lowered his head to shield his eyes from the midday sun. As he dashed down the steps, he took two large strides, got out his car keys—and then stopped cold. The spot where he parked his big, blue, semi-refurbished 1978 Chevy Impala was empty.

"I parked it right here." Perplexed, he scanned both sides of the street but it was clearly gone. His hands turned into fists. "Who the hell stole my car?"

Replacement ran up next to him and smiled. "You have two choices: you can have a *really* long walk to Rockingham, or you can take me with you and I'll show you where I hid the car." She held up his backup set of keys and jingled them.

Jack looked up at the sky. She was a mix of infuriating and adorable. He huffed. "Fine, but I'm driving." He snatched the keys from her just in case she decided to argue.

Her smile spread from ear to ear as she turned and bounded around the corner toward the back of the building. Jack shook his head and followed.

"Jack?" Someone called his name from above.

He stopped and looked up to the second floor where his landlady, Mrs. Stevens, waved her handkerchief. She struggled to lean her hefty upper body out the open window.

"The Dixons finished moving out. I'll have the downstairs apartment all clean in a day or two, but the painters can't start until next Monday. They should be done a few days after that." Her bright red mane of hair bobbed back and forth.

He smiled. "Thanks, Mrs. Stevens. I appreciate it."

"Give Alice my love."

He nodded. After he realized Alice was homeless, he asked Mrs. Stevens about the larger two-bedroom apartment downstairs. It was an odd arrangement, sharing an apartment with a girl he wasn't dating. He wasn't sure how his foster mother would feel about it, but hoped she was grateful. After he told Mrs. Stevens his plan, she called him a chivalrous man in a hard world. Jack didn't think he was; he just couldn't stand the thought of Alice living in some shelter.

Jack watched Mrs. Stevens struggle back through the window. He waited a second to make sure she didn't need help getting her large frame back into the room. Once she was clear, he walked on.

When Jack turned the corner and saw Replacement leaning seductively against his old car, his eyes widened. She posed like a hostess on a game show who had the job of showing off the prize. Jack rubbed the back of his neck. Her posture was doing more to show off her features than the car's. He inhaled deeply and a faint smile crossed his face. Although he and Replacement never really lived under the same roof before, they'd been raised in the same foster home—years apart, of course. He'd long since moved out and been adopted when she'd come on the scene and lived at Aunt Haddie's foster home. When Jack went back to visit Aunt Haddie and his best friend Chandler, Replacement was always there, following him around like a lovesick puppy. She'd had a crush on him then, and it hadn't seemed to fade over time.

The two of them sharing an apartment was easier than he'd thought it would be. He liked her.

"And the winner of the 'Locate Your Own Car' contest is…Jack Stratton!" She tossed her hands over her head and clapped.

"That's the prize?" he said dryly. "I won my own car?"

She smiled.

As he walked forward, he scanned the back alley.

Clear.

His years in the army and as a police officer had changed him. Now something as mundane as walking into a new area generated instinctive responses. He could no longer simply go somewhere—now he was always on patrol.

Head on a swivel. Look for anything out of place. Identify possible threats. Drive yourself crazy.

"Not only did you win the car, but you also get the company of the beautiful hostess."

"Great," Jack grumbled. "Now get in." The corner of his mouth curled up but he tried to hide his smile.

Replacement ran around, slid into the passenger seat, and flashed Jack a big grin. As he looked at her still bruised face, he realized how tough she was. The last traces of black and blue from her black eye were fading. There was still the slightest yellowish discoloration along her jawline, but that would disappear in another week or so.

Jack looked at his own reflection in the rearview mirror. The last month hadn't been kind to him, either. He looked rough. He was glad to get away and try to forget what both of them had just been through. He let the engine warm up for a few seconds, and then slid the seat back to accommodate his large frame. The Impala purred deeply. He gave her a little gas and then backed out.

They rode along in silence until they pulled onto the highway. He liked that about Replacement. She loved to talk but, unlike most girls, she didn't think it was the end of the world if he asked her to be quiet. Silence for them wasn't usually a bad thing; however, today it felt off. It was going to be a three-hour drive, but that wasn't the reason for the silence. Jack didn't look at her; he knew she was devising a way to ask him for the umpteenth time whether he really wanted to go through with this.

I don't want to go. It's the last place I want to go. I don't want to see her.

That was another change in his life. Before, his anger and bitterness kept his mother out of his thoughts. Now he had dreams about her every night. It had been almost twenty years since he last saw her, but lately she haunted him. Long blonde hair, clear blue eyes—she was beautiful; in his mind, she remained unchanged by time. He wondered what she looked like now. He pressed on the gas.

Replacement pulled her legs up underneath herself. "Did you get any sleep last night?"

"Some. Maybe an hour. Sleep deprivation. Isn't that how they torture people?"

Replacement's voice was slightly higher than normal. "I can drive. You can sleep on the way."

"I'm good, kid."

"We can always stop overnight someplace or something." Her voice rose nervously.

"Seriously, I'm fine." He looked over at her and noticed the trees whizzing by outside her window. He turned back and looked down at the speedometer.

Ninety-five mph. He took his foot off the gas. *Yeah...I'm fine.*

Replacement let go of her death grip on the door handle. "Just let me know if you want me to drive." She made the offer with a strained smile. The awkward silence took over once again. It was the kind of uncomfortable void where both people wanted to talk but neither knew what to say or where to begin. It was the kind of quiet Jack hated, but the only way to stop it was for him to say something, and right now that option seemed less desirable.

Replacement sat up and folded her hands in her lap. "We'll just go out there and see what happens. It'll be okay." She finished the pep talk with a quick nod of her head.

"Okay? We're going to a mental hospital. How 'okay' is this going to be?" His lead foot kicked in again. Cars pulled over to get out of his way.

Replacement frowned, pulled her legs up on the seat, and put her chin on her knees. "What should I call her?" Replacement's nose crinkled and she tilted her head. "Patricia? Ms. Cole? Patty?"

"Patty?" Jack shook his head. "I don't know. I don't know what I'm going to call her, let alone what you should." He took his foot off the gas and tried to slow down. "I can't call her…"

"Mom?" Replacement lifted her head off her legs. "Why not?"

"Because she threw that title away."

After a few minutes, Jack heard the wind between the Impala and the guardrail streaking by again. He looked down at the speedometer.

Ninety-eight. Damn. He took his foot off the gas and moved into the slow lane.

"I don't have any clue what I'm going to say to her. I haven't seen her since I was seven. Besides," he continued, "the doctor said she's not all there. She was a hooker and a drug addict for twenty years. That had to take a toll on her. I should feel pity or something…but I don't." Jack cracked his knuckles. "You're not supposed to hate your mother. I didn't at first because I didn't know enough to hate her. I thought all that crazy stuff was normal. After I was adopted, I got to see how a mother was supposed to act. The more I learned what a mom should be, the more I realized how bad mine was. That's when the hate started. The more love my new mom showed me, the more I hated Patty."

"I'm sorry." Replacement turned to look out her window.

Jack leaned back and drove with one hand on the wheel; the other rested on top of the seat back. Occasionally he had to force himself to slow down and back off the bumper of the rare car that didn't get out of his way. After two hours of silence, Replacement looked as if she were about to crack up. "Can I ask some questions?" She timidly looked at him.

"About what?"

"You growing up. What do you remember about your mom?"

Jack shuddered. "Sometimes I wished I could forget. Nothing good."

"Nothing? Not even one nice memory?"

Jack forced himself to focus on the road. "I think I blocked out those times. At least that's what a couple shrinks told me. They asked me the same question. There had to be something good, right? I remember slaps. I remember screaming." Jack breathed out. "The weird thing, though…those parts weren't the worst. She was actually paying attention to me then, so it wasn't so bad." He glanced at Replacement. "Screwed up, huh?"

"Yeah," she said quietly toward the window.

Jack rolled down his window to let the air sting him in the face. He leaned his head over and inhaled. After a moment, he sat up and shook his head.

"There were times when she would have a 'party' with a man and she'd have to find someplace for me to go. She used to work out a deal with the landlord who ran our tenement. I would end up stuck in the janitor's closet. It sucked. It was like getting solitary confinement, but I was five and I didn't know any better. It was worse when I was all alone—when I didn't know if she was coming back or…"

Jack arched his back and flexed his hand. His chest muscles tightened as he thought of the memory.

Replacement's lips pressed together. She shook her head. "I never realized how screwed up you had it."

Jack scoffed. "Thanks."

Replacement settled back into her seat and put her feet back on the dash. After another couple of miles, Jack clicked his tongue.

"What?" Replacement turned away from the window.

"I just thought of something…I wonder if I can find out my real name?"

Replacement nodded. "I couldn't find out your real name online. You're just listed as 'boy.' Stratton is your adoptive parents' last name, right?"

"Yeah. But I don't know my real first name." His eyes followed along the lines in the road. "She just called me kid or brat or moron, usually with swears attached to the front and back. Because of all the drugs, she probably forgot it herself."

"Your mother?"

Jack cringed and then nodded. "Yeah. So I named myself."

"Why did you pick Jack?" Replacement tried to smile but Jack could see hurt reflected in her eyes.

"It was the last thing she said to me: 'You don't know jack, kid.'"

Replacement inhaled but she didn't turn away. She blinked a couple of times and a tear hung off her lashes.

"Jack. To me it meant—nothing. You know the expression? You don't know jack. It means you don't know anything. And that's what I was…nothing."

"You're not nothing."

He looked over at her. "Thanks. I gave myself my middle name, too."

"Aunt Haddie is very proud that you picked Alton to honor her husband."

"Aunt Haddie was the best foster mother in the world." He gripped the steering wheel with one hand, looked over at her, and decided to joke. "She did okay with you, too."

"Okay? I was the pick of the litter." Replacement made a goofy face.

Jack searched Replacement's eyes for some clue... Aunt Haddie had known Jack's whole backstory. But she still said that Replacement had it harder than him growing up. Jack shuddered at that thought. He wondered what had happened to her.

Jack tried to drive the list of "what could be worse" out of his head and concentrated on the road.

"What about your father?" Replacement asked.

"Father? Whoever got Patty pregnant is about as much a father to me as that sign." He tipped his head to the speed limit sign that shook as they shot past it. "She never mentioned him. I doubt she knew who he was and I never cared."

Replacement swallowed and turned her head toward her window.

Jack slowly burned. He didn't like lying to Replacement but he didn't want to admit it to himself. He thought of his father every day. The older he got, the more he did.

The miles slowly went by. Jack rolled the window three-quarters of the way up. As he listened to the car's tires echo against the guardrail, he scanned the objects that had collected on the side of the road: bags, old tires, a baseball hat. The hat triggered a memory. It bothered him.

Did it just blow off someone's head or was it tossed aside? What am I, then? Could she not hold on to me or did she throw me out?

The guardrail ended, and Jack stared at the road.

Either way, it's trash now... just like me.

Jack felt the familiar burn of shame in his chest. His lips pressed together, and his throat tightened.

Why do I keep doing this...thinking about her? It was so long ago, but I can't get what happened out of my head. I shouldn't let any of that junk define me, but I still do. I'm driving in circles, caught in some loop that I can't break out of. I want to know why she abandoned me...but some things, I guess, I'll never know...

CHAPTER 2

Thanks For Scaring Me

They turned off the highway, and Jack flexed his hands. They hurt. He must have had a death grip on the steering wheel. The off-ramp led to a commercial section outside of the cute little postcard town they'd just passed. Homes with manicured lawns gave way to auto shops and supply companies. He slowed down as they drove past an empty shipping facility and turned onto a long curving driveway.

The mental hospital wasn't anything like Jack expected. He was anticipating a prison, but instead it looked like a large, brick school building. Three stories tall, the building was set far back from the road and the grounds were surrounded with a tall metal fence.

Jack stopped at the guard station. The older guard examined his license for a moment before he pressed a button that raised the bar that blocked the road.

Jack felt the low burn of adrenaline kick in. His eyes scanned the road as warily as they did in Iraq. Uneasiness washed over him as the building drew closer. His breathing sped up to catch his racing heartbeat. Somewhere in that building was the woman who held the answers to questions he had waited a lifetime to ask.

He thought about asking Replacement whether she wanted to wait in the car, but she hopped out before he turned the engine off. His heart pounded as if he were sprinting and he could feel the sweat on his back so he left his jacket in the back of the car. It was a short walk to the large granite steps in front of the building, but the brisk air did little to ease his anxiety.

"Everyplace has lepers." Jack muttered as he stared straight ahead. "They used to take them all and put them into one place, a leper colony."

"That Bible story freaked me out." Replacement shuddered. "Aunt Haddie read it to me and I didn't sleep."

"When she read it to me I got ticked off." Jack glanced over at her.

"Why?"

"Jesus healed ten lepers; only one came back and thanked him. One? Not a good return on his investment."

"I don't think he did it for that."

Jack shrugged.

"You know, I bet that one leper really appreciated it." Replacement stretched.

"Good point." He stopped and watched a patient being escorted by. He leaned closer to Replacement and fired off the words as if he were instructing a squad of soldiers. "Listen. Don't talk. Stay next to me. And *don't* get too close to anyone. Got it?"

"Keep your hands and feet inside the vehicle at all times." She flashed a huge smile.

"Seriously. These people can be dangerous."

"They could also be nice and just need some help. " She turned her hands out. "You told me yourself that everyone's a little crazy."

"There are different types of crazy," Jack whispered to Replacement. "There's the life-has-beat-me-down and I-have-a-problem-and-need-some-help type of mental illness. I feel bad for them. Hell, half the time I think I'm one of them. But there's also the Batman-Joker type of crazy. That type of crazy will kill you."

"Thanks for scaring me." She moved closer to Jack.

Jack held open one of the wooden double doors that led to a large intersection of two linoleum-tiled hallways. After speaking with three different nurses, filling out two separate forms, and showing their IDs four times, they were escorted upstairs.

They went through a heavy metal door that led to a long hallway. The left side had windows covered in mesh and bars that overlooked the front of the building; Jack could see the parking lot below. The right side of the hallway had large, thick, safety windows that allowed you to see through to an open common room.

Jack watched the men and women behind the glass. Some sat on couches, watching TV, or they sat at tables that were haphazardly scattered around the room. No one seemed to talk to anyone else. There were people talking in the corner, but they appeared to be talking to themselves.

Twenty-two people and six orderlies. One exit. Key card access. Guard nearest the door has a card. Jack squeezed his hand and forced himself to keep moving. *Think about what you're going to say to her and not how you'd escape if you were in here, stupid.*

They passed through a heavy steel door and sat on a padded bench in a corner of the third floor. Jack noted that on the first floor, they had nurses. Second floor, they had orderlies. Third floor, giant male orderlies. The mesh and the bars covering the windows made it clear this was the floor for patients who weren't too stable.

The man at the door was over six feet and weighed at least two hundred sixty pounds. He stood with his hands at his sides and smiled politely, but Jack saw his hard eyes; his main role was a guard.

A weary-looking man dressed in khaki pants and a white shirt headed their way. He looked to be in his thirties and was just slightly shorter than Jack. His collar was open, and he wore his blue tie loosely fastened around his neck. His worn-out appearance enhanced his worn-down expression.

"Doctor Vincent Jamison." He introduced himself and shook both their hands. "You're here to see Patricia?"

Jack nodded. "Thank you for letting me see her."

"Mr. Stratton, as I explained on the phone, Patricia has led a hard life. Unfortunately, that's taken a severe toll on her, both physically and mentally. She may not even recall you."

"I didn't think she'd recognize me."

The doctor cleared his throat. "I mean…she may not recall she even had a child. Her dementia is very similar to advanced Alzheimer's. She's gone weeks without even saying a word."

Replacement's expression saddened.

The doctor looked over at her. "There have been a few times, though, when she's been lucid."

Jack nodded.

She's not going to have a clue who the hell I am.

"We'll go in the room first," Dr. Jamison explained. "And then I'll have Patricia brought in."

Jack wiped his hands on his thighs. His mouth was dry, and his throat was tight.

Why do I need to do this? It's only going to hurt me more. Why open myself up again?

The doctor held the door open to a small room that had a table with two chairs on each side. There was a door on the other side of the room, and Jack couldn't take his eyes off it.

"Please, sit down." Jamison motioned to the chairs and walked over to the door.

The metal chair scraped across the floor, which caused Jack to involuntarily shudder. Cold sweat ran down his back. He wiped his hands on the front of his pants, but he never took his eyes off the door. The doctor opened it and spoke to someone, but Jack couldn't make out what was said. Jamison stepped aside, and then an old woman in a plain, blue dress walked through the door.

Jack stood up. There had been some mistake. His mother had long, blonde hair, not short gray hair that was thin and wispy. She was tall and fit, not frail and bony like the woman who hesitantly approached. Jack cleared his throat. "There must have been a mix-up—"

The old woman raised her head, and Jack saw those familiar blue eyes.

The years of drug abuse and prostitution had ground her body down to a shell of a woman. Her hand trembled as she leaned against the table as she sat down. Her head shook slightly with an almost constant tremor.

Jack had expected her to look twenty years older, but he was wrong. She didn't look as if she were in her mid-forties; she looked closer to seventy. He felt Replacement's hand take his. He didn't move. The woman who had haunted a thousand of his dreams sat only a few feet from him, but it was all wrong. In his mind, he always had had this conversation with the mother he remembered: a strong, beautiful young woman. He looked at this broken husk of a person. Anger clawed its way to the surface and burned inside him. Time had cheated him of the chance to confront the woman who scarred him for life. How could the woman who hurt him so deeply and the poor creature who rocked back and forth in a chair muttering possibly be the same person?

But it's her. This is my mother.

The doctor walked over and sat in the chair next to her. "Patricia?" She looked up, smiled at the doctor, and gave a quick spasmodic wave. "Some people are here to see you. We talked about it this morning." He nodded his head. She nodded her head, too, but Jack could see in her eyes she had no idea what he was talking about.

The doctor pointed toward Jack, and she turned to look at him for the first time. She smiled and gave him the same spastic, quick wave.

Nothing. No recognition. Wonderful. She doesn't know her own son.

Replacement squeezed his hand.

After a long minute, Jack finally said, "Hi."

Patty's face went white, and her eyes widened in a mix of terror and bewilderment. She raised a bony, trembling hand to her mouth. "Steven?" she gasped.

Steven? Is that my name?

His mother exhaled and let her hands fall into her lap. "You're okay. I'm so glad. I was so worried about you. How are you?" She leaned forward in her chair and smiled.

There was a long pause. Jack tried to smile, too, but he couldn't. He swallowed and slowly nodded his head. "I'm fine."

Patty nodded her head along with him. "You're fine? Really?"

"Yes. Thank you."

Her eyes narrowed, and then she leaned so close to Jack he wanted to slide his chair back. Her breath wafted across his skin in little puffs as she searched his face. Her head stopped going up and down, and she shook it side to side. "No...no, you're not."

"Patricia, this is your son," the doctor tried to explain.

"I had his son..." She nodded.

Had his son? She thinks I'm my father. Do I look like him?

"I tried to take care of him but..." She spoke to the doctor but didn't take her eyes off Jack. "I couldn't anymore. I..." She shook. "You're not fine." Her lips pulled back in a pained grimace. "You're dead."

The doctor placed a hand on her shoulder. "Patricia, it's okay."

"It's not okay. He's dead!" She thrust both hands at Jack.

Jack looked to the doctor. He just shrugged.

"I didn't know. I didn't know they were going to..." She stood up and the chair scraped loudly against the floor.

"Mom." Jack cringed when he said the word.

She moved back to the wall. "I didn't know they were going to be there. I didn't know that they'd hurt you. I didn't..." She started to cry hysterically.

The doctor looked at Jack as if to say "I'm sorry" and then raised his hand and waved to someone. Jack knew the orderlies would be there soon.

Jack stood up. "What happened?"

His mother covered her face. "Terry told me to get you to meet us. Sorry! I'm sorry... Please?" She moaned. "You... I came to the pond. You forgave me. You...love me. Why!"

"What happened? When?"

His mother sobbed and pushed herself into the wall. "It was… There was… Right after I found out about *it*. I didn't know what to do. I didn't know… You were so nice. Why would you…? You couldn't love me. No one could love me." She let out an enormous sob and started to hit the wall. "You're dead. They stabbed you…"

The orderlies rushed into the room. The doctor held out his hand to Patty. "It's okay."

She screamed, "No!" over and over, as if Satan himself had walked into the room.

Jack took a step forward. "Terry who? What's Terry's last name?"

Patty covered her ears with her hands. "Don't go there! Stay away from them." Her lips curled back in fear. "They'll kill you."

"I need to know. What happened?"

She wailed and pounded her fists against the wall.

The doctor motioned to the orderlies.

Jack looked away as the orderlies restrained her.

The doctor moved Jack toward the door. Replacement followed. The doctor led them back down the hallway. "I need to make sure she's alright." He turned and went back inside.

Jack stood—stunned.

"Jack?" Replacement took him by the hand.

"I need to go," Jack muttered.

She led him down the two flights of stairs, and past all the patients, nurses, and orderlies. When they reached the main doors, Jack pushed the big doors open and stumbled outside. He gasped for breath, like a drowning man whose head had just broken the surface of the water. He stopped and tried to breathe deeply.

Replacement rubbed his back. "It'll be okay," she whispered.

Jack closed his eyes. His words came out as a low growl. "How? How will it be okay? She's totally off-the-rails crazy and thinks I'm my father. She just said he's dead. Stabbed. How the hell's that going to be okay?" Jack stood up and pressed his hands against the sides of his head. He walked forward and looked back up at the third floor. "Did you hear her?"

Replacement nodded.

"That was just crazy talk, right? She's just nuts. Do you think…? I thought he wanted nothing to do with me." Jack looked at her. "Do you think my father's dead?"

CHAPTER 3

Home

Jack sat in the driver's seat, his hand frozen on the key. He stared straight ahead and didn't move. An old man in a tan work jacket got out of the car next to them. He was carrying a package of flowers and a cardboard box. There was a look of resolve on the man's face. Jack had seen that look a hundred times; it didn't matter whether it was a soldier going out on patrol or a policeman going on a raid, the look was the same.

It's called doing what you've gotta do no matter how much it sucks.

The man turned, and Jack watched him make the walk to the brick building.

"Jack?" she whispered.

"I'm thinking."

She put her hand on his. "Do you want me to drive?"

"No. What I want is some answers."

Replacement patted his arm.

Jack's head rose up. "Come on." He shoved the door open and headed back to the hospital.

"Jack?" Replacement hurried after him. "Jack, I don't think they'll let you talk to her again today."

Jack didn't turn around to answer her. "I need to talk to the doctor."

They headed back to the third floor and found the doctor speaking to an orderly. When Dr. Jamison turned and saw Jack, he sighed and rubbed his eyes. He whispered something to the orderly before he walked over to Jack.

"I'm sorry, Mr. Stratton, but—"

"I only have two questions." Jack held his hand up. "First, what she said about my father—did that actually happen? Or is she hallucinating?"

The doctor looked away, and his eyebrows knit together. "I can't be certain, but I think she was talking about an event that actually took place. When Patricia has spoken, which hasn't been often, she hasn't had any manifestations or hallucinations."

"Would it be possible for someone to monitor what she says from now on? Anything at all."

The doctor nodded. "I can pass that along."

"When will I be able to speak with her again?"

The doctor's face fell, and he looked at the floor. "That will need to be determined. As you witnessed, the visit was particularly traumatic."

"I understand. Do you know if I can talk to someone who has her case files? I need to find out her hometown."

"That I can help you with. The name of the town stuck in my head." The doctor adjusted his glasses and continued, "When I first met Patricia, she didn't speak for weeks. We were going through an identification game, and she started talking."

"Do you remember what she said?"

"We were going through pictures, and she yelled out, 'Alphie' and started clapping. I asked her about it, but I didn't get anywhere. I went back through the pictures, but she didn't respond. I asked her where Alphie was, and she said, 'Home—Hope Falls.' It sounded picturesque, so I looked up its location; it's just over the border."

"Hope Falls?"

"Yes. If I ever got a week off, I planned to go poke around up there."

"Thank you, Doctor." Jack shook his hand, and then he and Replacement headed back to the car.

"Jack?" Replacement hustled to catch up to him. "What are you planning on doing?"

Jack looked up the road. "I'm going home."

CHAPTER 4

Be A Good One

The traffic on the highway as they headed north toward Hope Falls was so heavy Jack had to stay in the right-hand lane. He drove with one hand on the steering wheel, with the window halfway down. Even with the sting from the cold air hitting him in the face, he had to force himself to pay attention to the car in front of him.

"Jack. I have a bad feeling about this."

"About what?"

"Going to Hope Falls."

Jack looked over at her.

"Whatever it was that happened up there freaked Patty out. Do you think we might be stirring up a hornet's nest?"

Jack looked out the window. "Part of me agrees with you. This guy Steven, he's probably a scumbag. What kind of man gets a prostitute pregnant? But...I need to know. I spent my whole life thinking the guy wanted nothing to do with me..." Jack's words trailed off as he saw the fork for the interstate ahead. He debated for only a second before he switched lanes. As they got onto the on-ramp to head to Hope Falls, his eyes locked with Replacement's. "I need to know."

She crossed her arms and sat back in the seat. "Count me in."

After fifty more miles, the interstate narrowed until it more resembled a sparsely populated main street than a highway. As they neared a gas station on the right, the low fuel light on the dashboard clicked on. Jack tapped the brakes and took a sharp turn in to the parking lot. He caught Replacement with his right arm as she slid forward.

"Doofus," she snapped.

Jack laughed. "I told you to wear your seat belt."

"That excuses you from driving like a wacko?"

He ignored her question. "I need something. Can you pump the gas?"

"We just got gas."

"It's an old car; I need a refueling plane following us. Just pump the gas."

"I'm a girl," she protested. "My hands will get all gassy."

"Gassy?" Jack stifled a laugh. "Fine," he huffed, got out and shut the door. Replacement smiled triumphantly and put her feet up on the dash. Jack shook his head.

He filled the tank and then ran into the little station. A big teenage boy was reading a thick book at the counter. Jack grabbed two sodas and some chips. As he headed back to the register, he noticed a map rack with a big sign above it that read "Take a Road Trip," with a picture of a highway stretching out into the distance. He picked one up and brought it to the counter. Then he tossed down some bills and grabbed a tin of mints.

"Will that be all, sir?" The clerk looked about eighteen and his black hair was pulled back in cornrows. He had a square face, and he pressed his lips lightly together.

Jack read his nametag: Titus.

"What're you studying, Titus?"

"Calculus." He gave his open book a push.

Jack looked at the coffee can that was labeled College Fund. "What're you majoring in at college?"

"Mathematics. I'm going to be a teacher."

"My father's a math teacher." He reached for his wallet. "A good friend of mine planned to be one, too." Jack smiled as he remembered Chandler. He snuck two twenty-dollar bills into the can.

Jack started for the door. As it opened, he looked back. "Do me a favor?"

"What?" Titus glanced up.

"Be a good one."

Titus smiled and nodded.

Jack jogged to the car, hopped in, and handed Replacement the map and a soda.

"Thank you. What's this?" She took a swig from her soda and held the map at arm's length.

"A map. Do you know how to read it?"

"Of course I know how to read a map. Why did you get it?"

Jack spoke mockingly: "So we can look at the *map* and find how to get to our destination."

Replacement took the same tone, but she slowed it down even further. "Or I could just use my smartphone with the built-in GPS?"

"Shut up."

Jack was backward when it came to technology, and he needed to catch up. His phone had a GPS, too, but he hated using it.

She tucked her legs up underneath her and pressed the screen on her phone.

Jack pulled the rearview mirror down and glanced at his reflection. "Do you think I look like him?"

"Like your father?"

"Did you see Patty's eyes when she saw me? Something in her clicked. She recognized me. Not me but my biological father. I always tried to guess what he looked like but I never guessed…me."

"He must have been a handsome guy." She pressed her lips together in a tight smile and glanced up at him.

Jack settled back into the seat and gave her a crooked grin. "Thanks."

Replacement looked at her phone. "It's a three-hour drive to Hope Falls."

"We'll have to find a hotel."

"Really? We'll stay in a hotel?" She sat bolt upright.

"Sure. Why not?"

"Awesome. Can I look for one? I've got this neat app I've been wanting to try."

"Yeah. We'll stop, get something to eat, and go to the hotel."

"You're going to check out her story? Maybe we can find something out there. When I tried to get information about you and your birth mother, it was killer hard. Nothing from back then has been digitized."

"Interesting choice of words: 'killer hard.'"

"Sorry." She kept pressing the screen on her phone. "There's a hotel right when we get off the highway. It'll be around eight o'clock, so we can get something to eat."

"Can you reserve a room with that thing?"

"Hold on." She tapped a few times and smiled. "Yep."

Jack looked over and shook his head. You'd think he was taking her to Disney World. As he slowed down for the car in front of him, he rolled his shoulders. Jack knew she grew up in foster care. She came to live at Aunt Haddie's when Chandler and he went into the army. Why couldn't she get placed? She was older for adoption, but she was like nine when she went into the system.

Jack looked over. "Can I ask you something personal?"

Replacement leaned in. "What?" Her face was so close to his that if he turned his head he'd be talking into her mouth.

He leaned his head away. "A little personal space, okay?"

"I brushed." She frowned. "Hey, I won't have a toothbrush."

"They have them."

"Who has them?"

"The hotel. Can you back up?"

She didn't. "Won't they cost a lot?"

"They're included." Jack turned to look at her with one eyebrow arched. "You've never…"

She turned red and scooted back over. "I never what?"

"Stayed in a hotel?"

"No. This is my first time." She smiled crookedly and played with her phone for a moment before she continued, "Was that what you were going to ask me?"

What the hell am I going to say? I want to know why no one adopted you. You look like a normal kid, so why did you get passed over? "I'm thinking that we will need…some stuff. A change of clothes. Can that magic device find a Walmart?"

"Really? Sweet! Yeah, hold on."

They crossed over the state line and a siren clicked on behind them. Blue lights filled Jack's rearview mirror. "Great," Jack muttered as he pulled over to the shoulder of the road.

Replacement's head bounced up and down slightly.

"Don't say it," Jack grumbled.

After several minutes of waiting, Replacement looked back. "I kept trying to tell you to slow down."

"Don't turn around."

"What's he doing?"

"He's running my plate. You want to call in the car to make sure nothing's flagged and see if everything is in line with the car and the driver."

Replacement's neck lengthened. "You have no idea who you pull over when you go up to a car. That's so dangerous."

Jack nodded. "I wish more people understood that. We could be pulling over someone who's late to get home to dinner or someone who just killed five people. Here he comes. Let me do the talking." Jack rolled down his window as the state trooper approached the car.

The trooper was five foot six with wide shoulders and a determined stride. His hat was pulled low so Jack couldn't see his face as he approached.

Jack opened his wallet and made sure that his badge was visible along with his license.

The trooper stopped beside the car, crossed his arms over his chest but kept his head down. "Are you blind or didn't you see the speed limit sign?" The trooper's voice was gruff.

"I saw the sign, sir, but…"

"But nothing. You saw that sign—you didn't see me. Did you, Stratton? Boom!" The trooper's arms swung wide and a huge grin spread across his face.

"No way…TANK!" Jack hurried out of the car.

The shorter trooper knuckle bumped Jack and then clamped both hands on his shoulders. "Look at you, Jack Stratton."

"What are you doing way out here?"

"I just transferred over to Rosemont. You?"

Jack hesitated. "I'm, ah…I'm heading to Hope Falls."

"Accompanied by a beautiful lady?" Tank winked at Replacement.

"Alice, this is Tank."

Tank leaned past Jack and thrust his hand out. "Jimmy Tanaka. Pleasure."

"Alice Campbell. Nice to meet you." Replacement nodded.

"She's Chandler's foster sister," Jack added.

Tank stood up straighter and paused for a moment. "It was an honor to serve with your brother. He was a good friend."

"Thank you."

Tank turned to Jack. "I'm trying to get some of the guys together. Are you still in Darrington?"

Jack nodded. "Yeah. If you do, I'm in. Just let me know."

"Great. I better move. I'm already late to report in."

"Good seeing you." Jack opened his door.

"Nice to meet you." Tank nodded to Replacement and then turned back to Jack. "I don't know if you get out here in the sticks much but you want to slow down. Locals out here are a tight-knit group. You won't make a good impression if you come into town like a bat outta hell."

CHAPTER 5

It is to Me

Replacement located a Walmart store three exits before Hope Falls. The plan was to eat quickly, grab necessities at Walmart, and then hit the hotel. Out in the woods, Jack liked to make camp first and then get the little stuff done. The problem was they had no gear. He made a mental list of what they needed for an extended stay. It wasn't a long list. People always overthink what they really need, but Jack figured he could get by with a lot less.

A little old lady with a blue apron and a kindly smile waved as they entered. Jack grabbed a shopping cart. Replacement took a sticker from the greeter and put it on her jacket like a badge of pride. "Where do we start?" She got up on her tiptoes and looked out over the massive store.

"I'll grab some stuff and meet you in the women's department." Jack snatched another cart.

Replacement pouted. "Can't we shop together?"

Jack rolled his eyes. "I hate shopping. Let's do this fast."

She shook her head. "Why do men hate shopping?"

Jack quickly pushed his cart in the other direction and headed to sporting goods first, where he grabbed a duffel bag. In menswear, he grabbed three casual T-shirts and a pair of jeans. He didn't need shoes, but he grabbed socks, underwear, and sweats before he headed to meet Replacement.

She was already walking toward him and grinned as if she had hit the lottery. She held up a tan shirt and a pair of jeans. "Is this okay? They're new."

"Of course they're new."

She looked hurt.

Jack's shoulders lowered. *You're a jackass, Jack. She's used to Salvation Army and secondhand. To her, this is a big step up. Look at her. She's like a little kid at Christmas.*

"That's not what I meant. They're great, but you'll need more. Come on." Jack headed back to the women's department.

"I got my outfit," she protested. "Don't you like it?"

"I do, but we may be there for a while, though. You need at least five outfits."

"Five!"

"You weren't planning on wearing the same clothes every day, were you?"

"I can't afford—"

"This is my outing. I got it covered, okay?"

As Replacement's eyes gazed at the cornucopia of products, Jack stopped to look at something. She rammed the cart right into the back of his ankle.

"Son of a—" He was about to let out a string of profanities when a little girl walked around the corner with her mother. He gritted his teeth as his eyes twitched.

The girl stuck out her tongue. He made a scary face back, and the girl ran to catch up with her mother. Jack pushed his cart with one hand and pulled Replacement's with the other as he limped over to the women's section.

"Sorry."

He gestured outward with both hands. "Go, seriously. You're helping me out, so I've got it. Get some more outfits. Five. You need a big T-shirt and some sweats too."

"A big T—why?"

"To sleep in."

"That's too much," she protested.

"No, it's not. Just get them."

Replacement looked at him with her big green eyes. He could tell that she was deciding whether he was serious. She raised herself up on her toes so she could search his face. He nodded his head, and then she flitted away. Jack watched her go to the clearance sections first, but at one rack, she paused and gazed at a beautiful brown dress with white trim. He watched her admire it and then she put it back on the rack.

After she went into the dressing room, he hurried over and pulled out the dress she liked. He stood there blankly and stared at size labels that made no sense to him.

How am I supposed to know her size?

He lifted one dress off, and held it up to himself. A guy walking by smiled. Jack awkwardly put the dress into his cart, and then scooped half the dresses off the rack and took them over to an older woman in a blue smock.

She raised an eyebrow as she looked at the pile of brown dresses on Jack's cart. "Can I help you, sir?"

Jack looked down at her nametag. "Barbara? Did you see the girl who went in there?" He pointed to the dressing rooms.

"The petite one?"

"Yes. Brown hair. Five foot four. Blue jeans and a light-brown jacket. She weighs approximately—"

"Am I arresting her?" She smiled.

Jack blushed. "What size do you think she is?" Jack gestured to the pile.

"Oh!" She thought for a moment and pulled out two of the dresses. "Have her try these on. One of them should fit."

Jack smiled and ran back to the dressing room. Replacement came out with four new outfits.

"I said five." Jack frowned but kept the dresses behind his back.

"How many outfits are you buying?" She tried to peek around him to see in his cart.

"I'm a guy." He held out the two dresses. "Here."

Replacement looked down at the dresses and froze.

Jack smiled.

She blinked a few times, looked up at Jack, and then burst into tears. It wasn't a little cry but a full-blown wail. She turned and dashed back into the dressing room, sobbing. Jack stood there with the dresses still in his arms. He looked helplessly at Barbara.

"Why don't you do some more shopping and let me handle this?" She patted his arm and picked up the dresses.

Jack nodded his head, turned, and walked in a random direction. He was already getting looks from various shoppers who were rubbernecking, trying to find the source of the noise.

What the hell was that? I thought the dress looked good.

Everyone was still looking at him, so he headed over to electronics, which was in view of the women's dressing rooms. Using a rack of DVDs for cover, he pretended to look at them while he waited. Barbara reappeared and glanced around. He hurried over to her.

She gave him a grandmotherly smile. "Everything's fine. She's just not used to someone being so nice to her. She told me how you've taken her in and all that you've done for her already. I think it's the kindest thing that you're getting another apartment so she can have a room and a bed. And now you've done this. She's very touched."

"Do you think she needs shoes to go with that dress?"

The elderly woman's eyes filled with tears, and she suddenly hugged Jack.

"You're the most thoughtful man."

Jack awkwardly kept his hand out as Barbara hugged him. *And women wonder why men don't like shopping.*

She turned, grabbed two different pairs of tan shoes, and disappeared into the dressing room. He crept forward and tried to listen. After a few seconds, Replacement started to cry again, and Jack's shoulders slumped.

"Why is she so moody?" Jack turned to look at the old man who'd spoken.

"What?" Jack asked.

"Is she pregnant?" the old man continued.

"Who?"

"Your wife?"

"No." Jack coughed and shook his head. "She's not my wife."

"Girlfriend?"

"Yeah. No. She's a girl...and my friend but...she's not my girlfriend."

"That explains it." The man nodded wisely, as if he'd solved a great riddle.

Jack rolled his eyes as he looked toward the exit and hoped this shopping trip would end soon.

Barbara came out and stood next to him. After a few seconds, she cleared her throat and the dressing room door opened. Jack's jaw dropped. Alice was so beautiful it took his breath away. She stood before him and just beamed. Her eyes were still moist with tears, but the smile on her face was contagious. Jack knew he grinned like a moron, but he couldn't help himself. Barbara nudged him from behind. He stepped forward.

"You look beautiful. Please, please don't cry anymore."

"You like it? Are you sure?" She looked down at the dress.

"Yeah…it looks great on you."

Barbara stepped over. "I'll have them ring it up in electronics so you can get going." She winked.

"Thanks for your help."

She nodded.

After they had checked out, Jack followed behind Replacement as she headed for the car. She varied between walking and skipping through the parking lot. She looked back at Jack and stopped. When he caught up to her, she gave him a quick hug and a gigantic grin.

"Thank you." Her voice cracked.

"It's nothing, kid."

"It is to me."

CHAPTER 6

Hope Falls

The Hope Falls Inn was a large, old estate home that had been converted to a bed-and-breakfast. Three stories tall, the enormous white house looked as though it belonged in a historical movie as it stood out against puffy white clouds and a bright blue sky. The plush green grass that surrounded the house was the kind that made you want to kick off your shoes and walk barefoot. Jack could tell by the new paint and manicured lawn someone cared very much for the place. He grabbed his duffel bag, and they started down the walkway.

Three wide steps led up to a wooden front porch with a white swing suspended on an ivory chain. Jack walked through the door and watched as Replacement turned around and took everything in. It was as if they were back in the 1800s. It didn't feel like a stuffy museum where nothing could be touched; rather, it felt like they'd stumbled through some time portal.

A middle-aged woman with brown hair swept up in a tight bun walked out of the doorway behind the main counter and came to the front desk. Like an actress walking onto the stage, her eyes scanned the room, checking to see that everything was in order. This stage was hers, and the guests were the audience. Adorned in a period-style dress with a high collar, she glided behind the counter. She lifted her chin, looked at Jack and froze. Her eyes widened. She only paused for a moment before she shook her head and gave a slight curtsy.

"Good evening," she said, in a polished and smooth voice with an 1800s period accent. "I'm Ms. Jenkins, and I welcome you to the Hope Falls Inn."

Jack smiled but there was something about the way she looked at him that caused him to stand up a little straighter. "Hello. We have a reservation. Stratton."

"Of course, Mr. Stratton. Room 102. It's at the top of the stairs and to the right." She smiled and pointed up the stairs. "The kitchen is closed, but if you're hungry I can get you something."

"No, thank you. We just ate." He signed the necessary paperwork and tossed the key to Replacement. She dashed up the stairs.

"Breakfast begins at seven."

"Thank you." He grabbed the duffel bag and jogged up the stairs after Replacement.

He stopped at the top of the stairs and looked back at the front desk.

Ms. Jenkins stood staring back up and watching him. Her eyes lifted slightly. "Will there be anything else, Mr. Stratton?"

"No, thank you." He turned, walked to the room and hurried in. The thirteen-by-twenty room was bigger than he expected and filled with all period furniture.

The wallpaper was a bright white with an intricate pattern of green filigree. A door on the right wall led to a bathroom; a door on the left led to another room at the inn. A large bed covered in a white comforter with fluffy, goose-down pillows, dominated the room. Dark ornamental bureaus stood along the wall, and a loveseat sat to the left of the door.

If you could travel back in time a hundred years, everything would have looked just like this.

He tossed the duffel bag down and then looked around for Replacement. She was gone.

"Hey, Alice?" he called out.

She walked out of the bathroom. "You were right. They have toothbrushes, toothpaste, shampoo."

"They do that." Jack tried to smile and not smirk.

Replacement held up a bottle. "I can't believe they give you all this for free."

Jack was going to explain that it was included in the price of the room but he didn't have the heart. He flopped down on the bed and groaned. "It's so soft. What's this thing made of?"

She hopped on with him. "I don't know but I'm going to *love* sleeping on this bed."

He sat bolt upright. "It's a king." He stood.

"Yeah." She grinned.

"You got a king?"

"Isn't it great?"

"No. Nope. Hold on." Jack walked briskly out the door, down to the front desk.

"Hi. I'm sorry, Ms. Jenkins, but there was a little mix-up with our room."

"How so?" Her smile vanished.

"There's only one bed."

"All of our rooms feature a full-size Victorian bed. That would be the most historically accurate, in keeping with our theme."

"All of the rooms?"

She nodded.

"Well, did they have a spare bed or a cot back in time?"

"I'm afraid not. There's a sofa."

Jack tried to recall the room. *Big canopy bed. Bathroom to the left. Old bureaus.*

"I can assure you that there's a sofa." She looked as though she was starting to get perturbed.

"Lady, do you have another room?"

"None of our rooms—"

Jack waved his hands to cut her off. "A whole new room. I'll rent two."

Her eyebrow rose slightly, and her blue eyes narrowed. "We're currently at full occupancy."

He put one hand on the counter and leaned in. "No offense, but is there another hotel in town?"

She smiled pleasantly and shook her head. "The nearest is in Plimpton, and that's a bit of a drive. I must mention that once you appear for your reservation, there are no refunds." She pointed to a sign behind the counter written in an old English script: NO REFUNDS.

"Is *that* historically accurate?" Jack leaned on the counter. "The Pilgrims didn't give refunds?"

Her jaw clenched slightly before she spoke. "The inn is designed to reflect the 1800s…"

"It was just a joke." Jack scowled, and so did the woman. He turned and started for the stairs. "Okay. Thanks. Thanks a lot." He wanted to stomp up the stairs, but he didn't.

Sleeping on the sofa won't kill me.

Jack marched back into the room and second-guessed his earlier assessment. The "sofa" was an old-fashioned loveseat that was four feet long. He sat down on it, and it moved under his weight. The white cushions were only about an inch thick. He rubbed them between his fingers, trying to figure out what they were stuffed with.

Hay?

Replacement stuck her head out of the bathroom and looked sheepishly at him. "Are we staying?"

"I guess so." He tried not to sneer.

"Can I take a bath? They have a giant tub. I could swim in it."

"Sure. Knock yourself out."

She let out a little squeal and disappeared. After an hour, she came back out, purring like a kitten. "Smell me! Smell me!" She ran over and thrust her hand under his nose.

Jack was going to protest the odd request, until he got a whiff. She smelled like lilies of the valley.

"It's nice."

"Feel!" Before he could stop her, she grabbed his hand and rubbed the palm up and down her arm.

He pulled his hand back. "Okay. Enough touching and smelling."

"What are you doing?" Replacement flopped down on the bed.

"Just making a to-do list." Jack circled the word LIBRARY.

"Where's my phone?"

"Over there." Jack pointed with the pen and a glowing red dot appeared on her phone.

"Sweet." Replacement held out her hand and let the laser pointer dot dance across her wiggling fingers. "That's cool."

"My dad's pen. He had it for teaching. I'm thinking about duct-taping it to my gun for a laser sight," Jack joked.

"Why don't you have one?"

"SWAT has them but Sheriff Collins won't allow them for field work. I like them but more as a deterrent."

"I think pointing a gun at someone would be a deterrent enough."

"You'd be surprised. Look at the difference." Jack aimed the pointer at her but kept it off. "Stop where you are!" He hammed it up and his voice shook along with his hand.

Replacement planted her feet and jokingly growled.

"Now." Jack's eyes narrowed and in his best Dirty Harry voice said, "Look at your chest, scumbag." Jack clicked the pointer on and the red dot pinpointed her heart.

Replacement grasped her chest. "Terminated." She flung her arms wide and collapsed onto the bed.

Jack laughed. "We better get to bed. I want to get an early start."

"I'm on the right." She giggled, dashed over, and got under the covers. When her head appeared, she snuggled down into the comforter and peered out at Jack. "You're not going to sleep on that?" She laughed as she noticed his blanket.

Here I'm trying to be nice about her screw-up, and she laughs at me?

"I know you didn't know better, but you should have gotten two beds." Jack plunked down on the sofa.

"Why? This one is enormous. You'll be all the way over there. Two beds wouldn't even fit in this room."

"I'm fine. I slept on worse in the army."

"But you don't have to. I don't mind."

"We're not sharing a bed. Go to sleep."

It was quiet for a couple of minutes and then she said, "Okeydokey. If you need to, just climb in on the left. I'll put pillows between us."

Jack smiled and lay back. He might as well have tried to sleep on a balance beam. The loveseat defeated him after an hour, but there was no way that he was going to get in the bed. There was a principle involved here. And seeing as how they were going to be roommates, he didn't want to start their nonphysical cohabitation off on the wrong foot. He wrapped himself in the blanket and lay down on the floor.

Jack rolled over and, as he lay on his back, he could feel his hair billow in a cold breeze. He couldn't tell where the wind came from, but a draft blew air steadily across the floor. He curled up tighter in the blanket. As the hours ticked by, he realized it wasn't the floor or the cold that kept him from sleep. He had dealt with far worse. It was the thought of what he'd face tomorrow that gnawed at his thoughts.

Jack rolled over and kept his eyes open. The nightmares were bad enough before.

What hell will I dream of tonight?

CHAPTER 7

Patty

Jack lay on his back on the floor and tried to let everything go. He closed his eyes and focused on his breathing. The rise and fall of his chest slowed as he imagined himself sinking into the floor. His muscles relaxed, and he finally drifted into sleep.

When Jack opened his eyes and looked around the room, it was a motel room but not the inn. It was the kind of motel he and his mother "lived in" when he was little. He looked down at his hands, and when he saw the Curious George doll clutched in them, he knew he must be dreaming. He hadn't seen that doll since he was five.

A little girl sat on the couch next to him. She sat there with her legs tucked underneath herself and stared at him. Somehow, he knew she was waiting for his answer, but he didn't know the question. He didn't know the girl, either. She was small and had big blue eyes. Her blonde hair was very dirty, but she had a bright pink ribbon in it.

"I'm five." She held her hand out, but she didn't smile. She just waited and stared at him.

Jack closed his eyes, but when he opened them, he was back in the institution. It was the room where he'd met his mother. The little girl sat across the table and continued to stare at him.

"Are you looking?" she whispered.

"For what?"

"You don't get it, do you?" She tilted her head and swung her legs.

"Don't get what?" Jack put his hand down on the table and shuddered—it was ice-cold.

When he looked up, the little girl held her arms against her chest and her lip trembled.

"Kid...don't cry." Jack forced a smile. "What's your name?"

"Patty." She held up her hand and it shook. "Stop looking."

"I need to find out what happened."

Her little shoulders rounded and her chin trembled. "Then you're going to die."

Jack's eyes flew open. He rolled over on the floor and found himself staring at the ceiling. He rubbed his throat and gulped for air as he fought to get control of his breathing.

From the amount of light coming in the window, he hoped it was past seven. He closed his eyes and lay there, listening for Replacement. He thought she was awake but he hoped he might get some more sleep. He'd gotten an hour, tops.

He heard Replacement roll over. Suddenly, Replacement threw back the covers, sprang out of bed and stepped on his stomach. She screamed and hopped back into bed.

"It's me," he grumbled.

Replacement stuck her head over the side of the bed. "Did you sleep on the floor?"

"No."

She tilted her head to the other side. "You're on the floor with blankets."

"Yes, I'm on the floor, but I didn't sleep."

"Oh, I'm sorry."

Jack groaned and got up.

"I slept like a baby. This bed is super soft."

"Let's go down to breakfast and then head to the library. I already took a shower."

"You took a shower in the middle of the night?" she asked.

"I thought it would help me sleep. It didn't."

"What's at the library?"

"Books." Jack smirked.

"I know *that*." Replacement bounded out of the bed and raced to the closet. "I don't know *why* you want to go there." She yanked open the door, reached into the closet, and pulled out the brown dress with the white trim. "Can I wear this?" She clutched it to her body and twirled back and forth.

"We're going to the library," Jack began, but when Replacement's smile collapsed into a frown, he quickly scrambled for words. "And I thought…you'd save that for dinner."

Replacement's smile exploded back on her face. She carefully hung the dress up and danced over to the bureau.

Boom. Nice save.

Jack stood there for several minutes while she picked up one outfit after the other and set them back down.

You have only five outfits to pick from, so pick one. Jack wanted to scream, but instead he sat down on the bed and waited. She finally settled on a blouse and a pair of jeans.

Jack lay back on the bed and let out a little moan. The bed was incredibly soft. He relaxed and let his hands roll out at his side. He inhaled deeply. The comforter's smell was familiar, but he couldn't place it. It smelled like spring. It wasn't an artificial scent like detergent or soap; it actually smelled like a warm spring day. He breathed in deeply and shut his eyes.

"Do you want to keep sleeping?" Replacement asked.

Jack's eyes fluttered open. Replacement was dressed but knelt on the bed next to him.

"I fell asleep." He shook his head and sat up.

"Only for a second. Isn't this bed the best?" She let herself fall forward and landed with a giggle.

"This bed rocks," he said.

"You can sleep if you want."

"No. No." Jack forced himself up. "I want to get to the library. But I'll warn you now, I'm going to be a bear. Let's go."

Replacement disappeared down the stairs, but Jack took his time. His sleep-deprived mood changed on a dime—it went straight to grim. He could almost feel the darkness inside him straining to get out. When his mother left him, he didn't deal with it well, according to all his therapists and ex-girlfriends. All the hurt, pain, and anger were like a beast that constantly attacked him and ripped him to pieces. He tried, but he couldn't wipe it out and he couldn't make it go away, so he dealt with the beast the only way he knew how: he caged it. He couldn't kill it, so he hid it away, building up layers and barriers to bury it.

Jack stopped at the top of the stairs and gripped the railing.

Why the hell am I here? I never should have come looking for her. She's freaking crazy. Is that why I'm so screwed up? Can you inherit crazy? My father must have been insane too. Who'd have slept with a girl like that?

"Mr. Stratton?" The innkeeper softly touched his arm, and his eyes flashed open.

"I'm sorry," he mumbled as he tried to get control of himself.

The expression on her face changed from slightly concerned to fearful as she looked at him. She took a step back.

Jack tried to smile, but his rage still burned. "I'm sorry. Excuse me." He turned and hurried down the stairs.

He took a right at the front desk and hurried over to the large room with four small, round tables and chairs set for breakfast. Jack stood in the doorway, but Replacement was nowhere to be seen. A young couple sat at the first table to the left. They were so close together, they practically sat in each other's laps. They were in their early twenties, and the girl kept her hand on the boy's thigh as they talked and stared into each other's eyes.

An open doorway was at the end of the room, on the right wall, and Jack assumed that was where the food was, confirmed by Replacement's appearance. She slowly walked into view, with both hands carefully holding a huge breakfast plate with a mountain of food. She looked up at him and grinned as if she'd caught a prizewinning fish. Jack motioned to the table nearest her, and they both sat down.

"You won't believe how much food they have in there," she gushed.

"Is there any left?"

"Tons. Pray. I can't wait to try this."

Jack bowed his head but sat there for a moment. "God…I…help me figure this out."

"That prayer stinks," Replacement mumbled as she took a gigantic bite of eggs.

"I don't think you're supposed to rate prayers."

Replacement moaned. "Why can't you rate a prayer? Help you? Is God your assistant?" She shoved another large forkful into her mouth. "These eggs are so good."

"I didn't mean it that way. I asked for help."

"You should say something like: 'God, show me the way.' You're just a tool that He'll use. And, you didn't say 'in Jesus's name.' I always end my prayers like that. I read it. 'Ask anything in my name.' That's what Aunt Haddie said Jesus told the disciples. Try this."

She stuck a slab of buttered brown bread into his mouth. He scrunched his face, but then he tasted it. The bread was delicious, and the butter had just a hint of honey. Jack's mouth watered, and Replacement nodded knowingly.

"It rocks, huh?" She smiled from ear to ear. "Aren't you going to get a plate?"

Jack laughed. "I thought you got enough for both of us."

Replacement put her arm on the table to block him while she pulled the plate closer to herself. "I wanted to try everything."

Jack got himself a plate of food. When he sat back down, Ms. Jenkins, the hostess from the front desk, appeared suddenly at his side.

"Is everything to your liking?" The look she gave him was odd; she opened her mouth as if she was about to ask something more but instead closed her lips in a tight smile.

Jack gave her a polite nod.

"This food is unbelievable." Replacement held up a forkful of what Jack supposed was an omelet.

"Thank you. We try our best to adhere to tradition, and all of the recipes and ingredients are historically accurate." Her graceful, floral dress had a slight scent of spring.

"The pancakes are the best I've ever had." Jack shifted in his seat.

"They're made with low-hanging blueberries. They just came into season. They tap the maple syrup on the farm down the road. Did you sleep well last night?"

"I did. That bed is so soft I could sleep all day. Jack slept on—" Replacement winced as Jack stepped on her foot.

"It was fine, thank you." Jack forced a smile.

The woman raised an eyebrow slightly. "If you need any information regarding the town or areas of interest, I'd be happy to be of service."

"Thank you. We did want to stop by the library. Could you give us directions?"

"Certainly. Please enjoy your breakfast. I'll write the directions down." She nodded her head slightly and backed away from the table.

Jack watched her turn and then walk to the desk. He hadn't realized how tall she was. She was only an inch or so shorter than he was. She looked back over her shoulder with a smile as she exited the room.

Jack grinned back.

Dancer. She must have been a dancer.

As he sat back down, Jack looked at Replacement, who made a face.

Jack smiled. Replacement had some filling from the crêpe on her cheek. He wanted to brush it off, but she looked too happy so he left it.

"Can I ask you something, and you promise not to laugh?" she asked.

Jack nodded, but he had no faith in his vow, considering how funny she looked.

"Can I take this with us?" She held up her plate.

Jack laughed.

CHAPTER 8

She Said "IT"

The library was set back from the road, tucked in behind a small high school. It was a two-story, square, brick building with a garden just outside. Just four cars were in the lot. Jack was grateful that the lights were on inside.

As Jack put the Impala into park, he leaned over to Replacement. "If they ask, we're here to do some historical research. It's a hobby."

"Got it." She smiled and hopped out.

Jack opened the door and hurried to catch up to her. "Just let me do the talking, okay?"

He held the wooden door open, and the stillness of the library enveloped them like an unseen mist. The room was beautiful. Old maple pillars reached up twenty feet to an arched ceiling. It looked as if someone had taken a sailing ship of old and turned it over.

Although the building itself was gorgeous, it was the feel of the building that reached Jack. It was perfectly quiet; the air was still but not stale. Jack breathed in deeply.

"It smells like the woods," he said, trying to whisper to Replacement, but he felt awkward speaking at all, as though he were disturbing some unseen force.

They slowly walked forward until they saw a woman behind a desk with a little plaque that said LIBRARIAN. She looked like a cross between a businesswoman and a waitress at a truck stop. The short, chubby woman must have been in her late forties, but it was hard to tell with all the makeup. She wore her light-brown hair high and with bangs in an 80s style that was frizzled and heavily processed. Her blue cotton blouse was a little too low-cut, especially for a librarian. She was merrily stamping books and didn't notice Jack and Replacement as they walked up to the long wooden counter.

"Oh!" She gave a little hop as she looked up at Jack. She looked down, gave her head a little shake and exhaled. "Why, you gave me a start." She smiled with her lips but not with her eyes. "Welcome to the Hope Falls Public Library. My name is Mae Tanner. How may I help you?"

"Good morning, Mae. My name is Jack."

Mae blushed as she shook his outstretched hand.

"I was wondering if you could help me," he said.

"I'd love to." She dashed around the counter and straightened her skirt. "Are you looking for something in particular?"

"Do you have a microfiche room?" Jack smiled.

"Why yes. Yes, we do. Right this way." She turned and hurried around a corner.

Jack rushed after her, almost dragging Replacement with him.

"Can't we try to look it up on the computer?" Replacement whined.

"Look up what, honey?" The librarian stopped so suddenly, Jack almost crashed into her.

"We're looking for some newspaper articles. Just the local newspaper for now. I'm sure it isn't online." He emphasized the last sentence, and cast a quick shut-up glare at Replacement.

"The local paper is online," Mae proudly proclaimed. "They started to publish online last year."

"That's great," Jack began, "but I wanted to look at some papers going back around twenty-eight years. We're here to do some historical research. Is that on microfiche?"

"It is." Mae turned and continued down the corridor to a side room.

Jack walked into a fifteen-by-fifteen room with old metal cabinets along every wall. In the middle of the room was a large wooden table with a microfiche machine.

"We have every copy of the *Hope Falls Times* since they started publishing in 1923. We also have the regional paper, the *Enterprise*. As you can see," she looked up at Jack and blinked rapidly, "we've also…we've also—" Mae stammered and looked down at her hands. "We also have—" She stopped again and cleared her throat.

"Mae." Jack placed a hand gently on her shoulder. "This is perfect." He smiled, and she started to breathe again. "This is exactly what I need."

"Really?" She smiled at Replacement. "Wonderful. Please let me know if you need anything else." She nodded and scurried out of the room.

Replacement stepped close to Jack. "What was that all about?"

"Shh…" Jack whispered as he peered out the door and watched Mae hurry back to her desk. "Maybe she's just nervous. Besides, this is what we came for."

"This? What're we going to find here?"

"First, we'll find out if my mother is just crazy and if any of what she said really happened." Jack walked over to the left wall. Above one of the cabinets was a banner that read: Hope Falls Press.

Jack pulled the cabinet open and grabbed the folders. When he turned back to the table, Replacement had already turned on the machine and was waiting for him.

"I'm twenty-six. She'd have been pregnant…twenty-eight years ago. We'll start there and go forward," Jack began. "Let me explain how this works."

Replacement, who sat on the desk, held up her smartphone. "Googled it. This reader has a translucent screen at the front, which projects an image from a microform. Three hundred pages per form, so I'm guessing one month per film." She gave a little wiggle when she finished and laughed.

"Show-off." Jack placed the folder down next to the machine.

"How do you know it happened before you were born?"

"When Patty was freaking out in the hospital, she said it happened after she found out about '*it.* '" His eyes burned, but his voice was cold.

"What does that mean?"

"The '*it*' she was talking about was me."

"I'm sorry, Jack."

Jack nodded and focused on his work. Starting with the January film, he put the square film into the machine, and the front page of the paper displayed on the monitor. "With a town as small as Hope Falls, a stabbing would be front page news, but just in case, we should check the whole paper," he said in a low, monotone voice.

They looked through every page but only found mundane stories about homecomings and elections.

February.

Every new page that appeared on the flickering machine made Jack's heart speed up. He forced himself to go slow and scan each page.

March.

Replacement didn't speak. She just pointed at the monitor once or twice.

April…nothing.

Jack put in the May film while Replacement watched over his shoulder. The machine hummed and the monitor glowed back to life.

When the page appeared, time stopped.

Replacement gasped.

Jack had never seen the teenager on the front of the paper, but he knew who he was looking at—his father.

"He was just a kid," Jack whispered. *Maybe seventeen. Smiling. Yearbook photo.*

"You look just like him."

Jack didn't move. His hand was frozen on the knob of the machine. He could hear his heart pound in his ears.

"Steven. Steven Ritter. That was my father's name. I was hoping she was wrong. That it was just some delusion…" Jack tried to read, but his vision blurred. "Teen Killed at Buckmaster Pond" was the headline of the article.

Jack scanned his father's face. Steven's photo was in black and white, but the resemblance to his own high school yearbook photo was uncanny.

"It says he was killed, stabbed… That's what my mother said… he was…" Jack wiped his eyes and turned toward Replacement. "I can't read it. Can you?"

She looked down at him with tears running down her own face.

"Jack…" She leaned down and wrapped her arms around him.

Jack shook. "I thought maybe…maybe she was just crazy. I always thought I'd meet him someday."

Replacement didn't say a word; she held him tighter.

"When I was a kid and things were tough, I thought he'd come looking for me, and save me." Jack's shoulders slumped.

"Oh, Jack."

"My father's dead."

Jack couldn't hold back his emotions any longer. Replacement held onto him and slowly rocked him back and forth. Jack had no idea how long he cried, but Replacement never let go of him.

After a while, he finally sat up and wiped his eyes. He looked out the door and saw the little librarian holding a box of tissues. Jack looked away while Replacement hurriedly went to the door.

Mae hesitantly stepped forward and held the tissue box out toward Replacement. Mae's head angled toward the large microfiche screen and the box tumbled from her hands.

"I'm sorry," Mae mumbled as she picked it up.

"It's okay." Replacement reached out for the box.

"Certainly." Mae hurried out of the room.

Replacement turned back to Jack.

"Thanks." Jack's voice was raspy. "Sorry I'm such a pansy."

Replacement lowered her face to eye level with his. "Shut up." Her lips pressed together. "You just found out your father was murdered."

Jack cracked his neck and stood up. He stretched and then walked toward the door.

Replacement's voice was soft. "Do you want to go?"

He reached down to grab a pencil and some scrap paper. "Leave?" Jack's voice was a low growl. "No. I'm just getting started."

CHAPTER 9

Acta Non Verba

Replacement and Jack sat side by side as he scanned through the main points of the first article.

"On May 13, an emergency call came in, reporting a stabbing at Buckmaster Pond. Steven Ritter. Seventeen. Beaten. Stabbed. No other information. Police following all leads, according to Chief Dennis Wilson."

Jack stopped and looked at Replacement, who wrote as fast as he spoke.

"We can come back," she offered.

"I'm fine." He turned to the monitor. "This is better for me. Really."

He scanned the article to see whether he'd missed anything. His hand turned the knob forward until he came to the next week's paper.

"Next article. May 20. Police are asking anyone with information to come forward. No suspects. No witnesses. Steven. Only child of Mrs. Mary Ritter, a widow…"

My grandmother. She was a widow.

Jack's fists shook on the table, and he knew he was close to smashing something. "I'm sorry. My head is going to explode. My crazy mother was right. And now I know my father is dead. Murdered. His father was already dead. My grandmother…she was…all alone."

"Jack. This is too much for anyone all at once. Let's go for today, okay? We'll come back tomorrow. We've waited this long. We can wait one more day."

"Wait another day? I don't want to give the guy who killed him another breath, let alone another day. Let's get a little more. Can you please drive?"

Replacement hesitated, but when Jack stood up, she moved over in front of the microfiche machine. "All right. Next article." Replacement began to read. "May 27. Police say there's still no progress. Following multiple leads. Cause of death: multiple sharp force injuries. Police asking for help. The police searched the area surrounding the pond, but no weapon was recovered."

"Does it give any other names? Cops' names who were involved in the investigation?"

Replacement scanned the article. "Frank Nelson and Henry Cooper. They're listed as responding officers."

Jack wrote it down.

"Next week." Replacement scanned the front page and frowned when she saw no mention of the murder. Page after page went by, but there wasn't a single reference to the crime. She looked at Jack, but he just stared at the paper. She quickly rose and put another month in the machine. She slowly turned the knob, but that month had nothing on the murder either.

"How quickly people forget." Replacement took her hand off the dial.

"They didn't even bring in the state police to dredge the pond. It froze over before they could get a dive team here. But what about spring? Did they just forget about him?"

After three months with no articles, Jack stood up. "We've gotten everything from the newspaper that we're going to get."

Replacement nodded, and then turned to put the folders back. Jack ran his fingers through his hair and sipped the water. He took another sip and closed the bottle. "One more stop and then we go."

The library was absolutely still as they walked back to the main desk. They passed a section of empty wooden desks. For just a flash of a moment, he could picture his father as a schoolboy sitting there, reading. Jack stumbled and stopped.

My father would have come here. He'd have...

His whole body tensed. He could see the look of concern on Replacement's face.

She turned and nervously looked at him.

"I'm fine. I'm just trying not to go down the 'what could have been' road."

"Don't go there." Replacement's voice was low. "It will make you crazy; then it will kill you."

Her words caused Jack to pause. He searched her eyes. Her face was stern and her gaze was steady. "Is that a road you've been on?"

She didn't answer him.

He gave a brief nod before he kept walking.

Jack headed over to the main desk; it was empty. Jack looked around but Mae was nowhere to be seen. Jack walked toward the corridors of books in the main room on the left. Replacement stayed just behind Jack, and he kept feeling her gently touch him on the back or pat his shoulder. Jack read the signs at the end of the shelves until he found what he was looking for— almanacs, yearbooks and handbooks. He went down that corridor, stopped in the middle and gestured to the section.

Replacement grabbed a step stool from the corridor and made Jack sit down. She scanned the shelf. Jack could see her counting.

"Go back thirty years and grab the books through twenty-five years ago to be on the safe side," he mumbled. She handed the stack of books to Jack, and he handed three back to her. "Look for my father's class first. I don't know if my mother's class was the same."

Replacement nodded and leafed through the pages.

Jack flipped through the photos until he landed on the Rs. "Got it."

He stared at the picture of his father. It was the same picture as the one in the paper, although this one was in color. Replacement leaned over his shoulder.

"You look so much alike. Look at his cheekbones and chin. But your eyes...they're the same. Totally."

Jack read the text below the photo. STEVEN RITTER. "ACTA NON VERBA" IN MEMORIUM. Puzzled, he looked up at Replacement, but she was typing on her phone.

"Acta non verba?" she repeated as she continued to type. "It's Latin. It means deeds, not words."

"I wonder if he picked it?"

Replacement took the yearbook and flipped to the Cs. "Marie Drake, Theresa Cook, Alyssa Connery." She read off the names until Jack's finger touched the page.

He stared down at the photo. His mother smiled from ear to ear. She had long blonde hair and was posed leaning against a tree. She wore a simple white dress, and she was beautiful. Jack squeezed the yearbook, and his eyes narrowed.

The yearbook text read, PATRICIA COLE, but underneath her name, someone had handwritten in pen the words, CLASS SLUT.

Jack's anger boiled.

"They were in the same class." Replacement took one of the scraps of paper and scribbled the info down.

"We need to look for a guy named Terry. She said Terry told her to get Steven to come to the pond. If you find one, flag the page. You start on the previous year."

"Do we know if Terry even went to her school?" Replacement held up her hands.

"No. We don't. I'm assuming."

They both flipped through pages. After a minute, Replacement blurted out, "Found one." She pointed to the page.

Jack looked at the picture. A young, smug-looking guy. Dark hair and brown eyes. TERRY BRADFORD.

"He'd have been a year older than my par—than them. Keep looking."

Replacement flagged the page and added to her notes. Jack kept scanning.

All these kids. They knew my father. I wonder…

He shut his eyes and tried to concentrate. His finger moved across every name before he flipped the page. At the Ms, he stopped.

"I've got two. Terry Martinez and Terry Martin."

"He looks like a jerk." Replacement poked Terry Martin's picture.

He was dressed in a football sweater with an open collar around his thick neck. Jack looked at the kid's cocky grin and wanted a chance to knock it off his face.

She pointed to Terry Martinez. "He looks nice. Nerdy, but nice."

Dressed in a white shirt and plain blue tie, he looked younger than the other students. He was thin, had a mop of black hair, and wore thick glasses that looked too big for his face.

The book's backing made a cracking sound as Jack's hand tightened around it. He relaxed his grip and continued to flip pages. Replacement quietly started again, too. After ten minutes, Jack got up, grabbed two more years, and handed one to Replacement. Neither of them found any reference to a Terry in the other yearbooks.

"It's a two-year window. We've got three guys named Terry. It's a place to start." Jack stood up and put the other yearbooks back on the shelf but held onto the ones he'd flagged. "We walked by a photocopier. I want to copy the pictures."

Replacement followed him back down the corridor to the machine. It wasn't the best quality, but after a couple minutes, he had his copies. Jack began to close the lid but stopped and sighed.

"Jack? What's wrong?"

"A world of pain I didn't know existed two days ago is making me crazy," is what Jack wanted to say, but instead he replied, "I think I should photocopy the whole book. There might be something in here."

"Can you check them out?"

"No. They're reference books. Don't sweat it. I gotta get out of here anyway. I need a break."

Replacement nodded and took the two yearbooks from Jack and ran back down the aisle.

Three names. How can I run background checks on them from here? I don't think I can connect to any of the police systems with a phone.

Jack kept his eyes closed as he pondered what course to take.

I could call Cindy and have her run a check on the QT. I doubt they had computers in the Revolutionary War, so the inn won't have one. They have one here, but—

When Replacement touched his arm, he jumped.

"Sorry." She smiled.

"Let's go. Are you hungry?" Jack asked.

"Starving." Replacement hugged her stomach.

"You just ate that humongous breakfast. How can you be starving?"

"It's almost three o'clock." She held up her hand. "But I don't have to get something—"

"I didn't realize it was so late. I'm sorry. Come on."

As they walked past the main desk, Mae was still nowhere in sight. Jack thought of calling out but quickly dismissed the idea. "We'll be back. We can thank her then," he whispered.

Jack walked out into the cool air, stopped, and breathed deeply twice.

Replacement grabbed his arm. "I'm driving." She pulled the keys from his pocket and darted around to the driver's side. "You look like hell."

"Thanks," Jack muttered, but he didn't protest her driving. "I feel like hell."

He closed the door and looked at Replacement, who squirmed in the driver's seat. Perplexed, he stared, thinking she must be trying to take her jacket off as she struggled with something behind her. She leaned forward; then, with a triumphant grin, she pulled two yearbooks from inside the back of her sweater.

"You stole the yearbooks?" Jack's mouth fell open.

"I didn't exactly steal them. You said there might be something that you need in them."

"There might be, but you took them."

"I did take them, but I didn't steal them because I'm going to return them."

Jack was about to argue but closed his mouth.

"Fine." Jack leaned against the window.

Replacement broke into a huge smile. "I'm glad you agree."

As Replacement pulled out of the parking lot, Jack saw the librarian standing at the side entrance, animatedly talking with a tall man. The man looked to be about Jack's age. He wore a worn baseball cap, tan work coat, jeans, and boots.

Mae noticed Jack driving away. She grabbed the man by the arm and pulled him inside the library.

"Where do you want to eat?" Replacement headed for the main road.

Jack looked away from the closed door and tried to drive his police officer paranoia out of his head. "Anywhere, klepto."

CHAPTER 10

Buttercup

They pulled up outside Bartlet's Family Restaurant; it was a large log cabin with a wide wraparound porch. Jack stretched as he opened the car door. He couldn't get over how warm the winter had been. A jacket was still needed, but for the beginning of February, it was a heat wave.

Quite a few cars were parked outside, so Jack hoped the food would be good. Replacement zipped up the wide, short steps and held the door open for him. The entrance to the restaurant was a spacious front room that doubled as a gift shop. Everything was either on a yellow pine shelf or in a pine barrel. They had many plastic toys for kids, crafts, shirts, and caps that lined the walls.

Jack turned around to look for Replacement, but she was nowhere to be seen. He walked back and found her examining a pink T-shirt with HOPE FALLS written in the middle of a large red heart. He grabbed her by the arm and headed for the hostess in the far corner.

"Can I look for a minute?" Replacement begged.

"You can look for an hour after we eat." Jack smiled. "Table for two," he said to the young woman who stood behind the wooden podium.

She smiled, grabbed some menus, and led them to a little corner booth. Replacement slid in and her mouth dropped open. Jack looked out the window to see what had made her so happy. Behind the restaurant was a small garden with a little natural waterfall in the back.

"Isn't it pretty?" their waitress remarked as she stopped beside their table. "I just love it. It's so romantic." She gave Replacement a little pat on the shoulder and winked.

"It's beautiful." Replacement kept gazing out the window.

Jack suddenly stood. "I'll be right back."

The waitress looked perplexed. "Do you want to order?"

"A burger and fries," Jack called over his shoulder as he marched back into the store. "And a Coke."

He walked into the gift shop again and scanned the shelves. He looked around a little but didn't see what he needed.

"Do you have any notebooks?" he asked the woman who had seated them.

"Yes, we do. Right here." She moved over and pointed to a section with two notebooks: a thin one covered in puffy baby farm animals and a thicker one in purple with sparkling confetti and "HOPE FALLS" written in pink.

Jack rolled his eyes and paid for the thicker notebook, along with a pen.

"She'll love them," the woman confidently assured him.

"Who will?"

"Your girlfriend." She smiled.

Jack tilted his head down, grabbed the bag and hurried back to the table. Replacement looked out the window as he slid back into the booth.

"Where did you go?"

"I needed to get a notebook." He put it on the table.

She snickered. "Pink's not your color."

Jack's eyes narrowed. "What're you, five years old?"

"Me? I'm not the one with the Pretty Pony notebook."

"Anyway," he pulled out the notes from his pocket, "I figured we could get started organizing the information we have."

"I'll write." She took the pen.

They spent the next hour eating while they transcribed the notes. Once they had everything written down, Jack frowned. "We don't have much."

"It's a good start." Replacement slurped down the last of her milkshake and ended it with a loud smack of her lips.

"There wasn't much concern in the paper."

"There was at the beginning."

"The story faded out fast."

They settled into an awkward silence. After a few minutes, Jack stood. As he went to pay the bill, Replacement headed back to the little shop. After he paid, he swept the perimeter to look for her, and located her back at the pink shirt she had admired before. She looked at him, hopeful.

He grabbed a matching pink baseball hat off the shelf. "Get the hat, too."

"Really? No. I don't want to spend—"

"Get them. They'll look good on you."

Replacement tried to hide her blush as she took the shirt off the rack.

"Come on. I want to make one stop before we head back to the inn." Jack moved to the register.

"Where?"

"There was a little general store in town. I'm hoping they have what I need."

"You're not gonna tell me?" She walked up next to him.

"It's none of your business." Jack took the shirt and hat and handed them over to the cashier. "Just these."

"Did your girlfriend like the notebook?" The lady smiled toward Replacement.

"What? No, she's not..." Jack winced when Replacement pinched him.

"He's such a kidder." Her arm slid around Jack's waist, and she gave him a hard hug. "Thanks, sweetie. I loved my notebook."

"Sure...buttercup." Jack pinched her cheek. "Let's go."

He smirked and headed for the door as Replacement hurried to catch up.

"Buttercup?" she whispered. "Come on. You stink at being undercover."

"Don't start the whole undercover thing again."

"What do you mean? I did great undercover."

"We're not undercover." Jack's voice got louder as they walked out of the building and toward the car.

"Are we telling people what we're doing?" Replacement looked perplexed.

"No."

"Ha!" She pointed a finger in his face. "Then we're undercover."

"No, we're just not…" Jack pulled open his door and leaned on the roof of the car as Replacement walked to her side. "Fine. We're undercover. But we're not doing the boyfriend-girlfriend thing."

"That's our cover. You can't be undercover unless you have a cover, and that's our cover."

"We can pick another cover." Jack frowned.

"No, we can't."

Jack shook his head.

"What would we pick? We're really a traveling circus team?" Replacement pantomimed juggling.

Jack tried not to, but he smiled at her joke as they got into the car. "No. We keep it simple and vague. We're doing some historical research. It gives us an opening. Then we wait and see what they say."

Replacement crossed her arms.

"You don't like that plan?"

"I don't like any of this. We're going after the man who killed your father. He's dangerous."

Jack started the Impala and the engine roared. He looked over at Replacement. He wanted to reassure her that she was safe but when the words came out of his mouth, he could see the fear they produced in her face. "So am I."

CHAPTER 11

Traveling Circus

Jack pulled over at the general store in the center of town. It was the largest building on the block, and employees were bringing in the miscellaneous items they'd set out for display earlier in the day. As he turned the car off, he watched a family walk down the sidewalk.

A young boy tugged at his father's arm. The man had his other arm around his pregnant wife, who smiled and waved to a car that passed.

This would have been my hometown. It's like Mayberry. I would have grown up here.

The leather on the steering wheel creaked as his grip tightened and Jack shut his eyes. He wanted to smash something to keep from feeling anything. He flung open his door and jumped out of the car.

Replacement hurried after him as he marched to the door. He pulled the glass door open and a little bell rang overhead. Row upon row of neatly stocked shelves filled the right section. Racks of clothes were on the left. The checkout was in the back of the store. It was a throwback to a more innocent age when people were trusted.

A few shoppers were scattered around the store, but he was looking for an employee. A young girl with a red apron stocked some shelves. She stopped as Jack approached.

"Can I help you?" She was maybe sixteen, with blonde pigtails, braces, and a warm smile.

"I need an air mattress."

"We have that." The girl spun around and walked down the aisle. As she searched the shelves, she held her finger out in front of her like a pointer.

"Nope…no…it was…here," she proclaimed as she located the one faded box. "Are you using it for sleeping?"

Jack blinked a couple of times and tried not to smirk. "Actually, I'm with a traveling circus and we need it because our net broke."

The girl's eyes became saucers. "Really?"

Jacked laughed. The girl kept smiling, waiting for him to elaborate.

He laughed again, louder. "I'm sorry. I just—"

The girl jumped as a loud pop followed by the tinkle of broken glass echoed behind them. Jack turned to see an old woman frozen in place. Her hands were out in front of her. Whatever she'd been holding lay in a million pieces on the floor. Jack glanced at her face. He couldn't place the emotions that raced across her eyes. *Fear. Confusion. Warmth.*

"Are you okay?" Jack moved the clerk to the side and slowly approached the woman. "You should back up a little away from the glass."

The woman grew paler. Her trembling, gnarled hand reached up to her mouth while the other cinched her jacket tighter to her chest. She stepped forward; her feet crunched the glass on the floor.

Jack angled his head and tried to smile as he reached out to steady her. She didn't take his outstretched hand. Instead, her hand touched the side of his face as she moved even closer. The woman must have been in her seventies. She was very small and slightly hunched over. Her white hair was short and wispy, but her blue eyes were bright and now glistened with tears.

"Do I know your parents?" The woman's voice was a whisper.

Jack swallowed. He opened his mouth and closed it again.

"Mrs. Ritter? Mrs. Ritter!" An older man with a red apron rushed down the aisle toward them.

She didn't take her eyes from Jack's face. She smiled at him, and a large tear ran down her wrinkled cheek.

Jack stepped back. "I'm not from around here."

The old woman's lip trembled, and her hand fell back to her side.

"I'm sorry, sir." The clerk put his arm around her shoulder.

Jack grabbed the mattress box and bolted for the checkout. As he stormed by, Replacement reached out for his arm, but he didn't slow down; he marched to the checkout counter and quickly counted out the bills.

"Jack…"

"Don't. I can't…" He glanced over his shoulder and then shook his head. "Not right now."

The clerk handed him the receipt.

Jack kept his eyes on the floor as he retreated to the car. Replacement's door had barely closed when Jack whipped the Impala out of the space. His face was white, and his jaw was set.

"Jack…"

"Don't."

"She's your grandmother."

"You don't know that." He smacked the steering wheel. "My mother was a prostitute. How do I know that Steven Ritter even was my father?"

"Jack. Come on."

Jack glared straight ahead. Jack took a right and just drove. He wanted to put as much distance between him and the store as quickly as possible.

Replacement put her feet flat on the floor, closed her eyes and whispered, "Jack, you know he's your fa—"

"You don't know. I doubt Patty knew who the real father was. He could have been a hundred different guys."

"Look at that picture. He looks just like you." She scanned his face, the look of confusion evident on her own. "Why are you running away?"

Jack's teeth ground together. "Even if he was, so what? He was probably as crazy as her. He dated a whore. What kind of man—"

"He was seventeen." Replacement cut him off. "Maybe he was nice." She looked down at her hands. "Maybe he was like you."

"Like me?" Jack scoffed. "You don't know him. You don't know me."

He stepped on the gas, and the Impala raced forward.

"I know you." She spun on the seat to stare at him.

"No, you don't." He slammed on the brakes at the red light. "Be glad you don't."

"I do know you. Michelle talked about you all the time."

"That's different. That's the outside. She told you about what I was doing, or stuff we did when we were little. She didn't tell you about me." He pointed at his head. "Stuff in here."

Replacement's voice lowered. "She told me about here." She pointed to his heart.

"She wouldn't have told you. Not about…personal things." Jack froze. He stared at the dashboard and the hairs on the back of his neck rose with his breathing.

"She was worried about you," Replacement whispered.

"Did she…? Damn it," he snarled.

"We were like sisters." Replacement pulled her legs up and hugged them.

Jack's anger swirled the silence into an uncomfortable void between them.

"That's a reason for her to break my confidence? What did…?"

Jack's mind raced. He had confided everything about himself to Michelle. To him, it was so odd. She was two years younger than he was, but ever since they were kids, she'd been his confidant and advisor.

"After Chandler died…you didn't come back, and she didn't know what was going on with you. Michelle was hurting too, and I think talking about you helped her. She was worried so…we talked."

I told Michelle everything. All of it. Did she tell Replacement…everything?

Jack stomped the accelerator as the light turned green. The Impala's rear tires spun for a second before the car shot forward. Jack snarled. "That doesn't mean you know me."

Replacement looked out the window. After a moment, she spoke, and her voice was flat. "You know nothing about me, Jack."

The realization that she was right hit him in the throat. He caught his breath, and his foot eased off the gas. Over the last couple of months, he could only remember a half-dozen moments when Replacement was at Aunt Haddie's.

Aunt Haddie brought her home when she was, like, eleven. Her real name is Alice, but she doesn't like it. Why? What happened to her parents?

The list of unanswered questions was long. He glanced over at her, and she was still pensively looking out the window. *Was she thinking about the same things? Her parents? Her past?* She didn't look over in his direction, and he couldn't blame her.

She's right. Ever since she showed up in my living room, what have I learned about her? She saved my life and I treat her like everyone else. I keep her out. I don't want her to know about me, and I don't know anything about her.

Jack stopped at another light and watched the cars slowly pass.

I take her into my life but I keep her at a distance. Jack, you're a piece of work.

"I'm sorry." His words hung in the air, but she didn't turn her head. "You're right. I don't know anything about you, either."

He heard her exhale, and she put her feet on the floor. Her voice was soft but clear as she spoke. "I think you're wrong, Jack. Steven Ritter was your father."

Jack pulled over and shut the car off but kept looking straight ahead.

"I know. I knew it when I saw the photo." Jack looked out his window. "As long as I can remember, I've always wondered who my father was. I'd be somewhere, see some man who looks sort of like me, and think maybe he's my dad... It drove me crazy, but I couldn't stop doing it. I mean, I'd be arresting some guy, and I'd be thinking: could this be my father?"

Jack ran his hands through his hair, and then shook his head. "Now I find him and...I want to deny it. I want to say it's not him. It's some other guy but not him. That's why I couldn't say anything to Mrs. Ritter. I'd be admitting what I know. Steven Ritter was my father. And he's dead." Jack leaned his head back. "I just didn't want it to be him. How's that for crazy?"

Rain fell on the windshield and dinged off the roof.

"Jack, that's not crazy—it's normal."

"Crazy is the new black?"

"No, but anyone can understand why you wouldn't want it to be him." Her voice was as soft as a cloud as she spoke the words. "I'm sorry your dad is gone."

"Me too."

CHAPTER 12

My Turn

The light rain turned into a downpour. The gray cloud cover had changed to black. Jack felt it in his bones——a storm was coming.

The parking lot was a short walk from the inn so they ran through the downpour for the porch. They were both soaked by the time they reached the top of the stairs. The cold rain seemed to invigorate Replacement, and she grinned broadly. It had the opposite effect on Jack. The chill felt as if it sucked the warmth and strength right out of him. He leaned against the wall.

"I'll be one second." He pulled out his cell phone and held it up.

"I'll wait." Replacement smiled and leaned against the wall next to him.

"You're soaked. Why don't you run up and take a bath?"

Replacement grabbed his jacket and pulled his face closer to hers. "Do you know how good that will feel?" Her whole body vibrated.

He smiled. "Go. Enjoy yourself," Jack encouraged her.

She hummed a little tune and happily rushed off upstairs. Jack smiled, but a cold gust of wind and an icy spray of rain quickly extinguished any of the joy left from Replacement's enthusiasm. He turned to the wall, pulled out his phone and called Cindy.

"Hello, Cindy Grant speaking."

"Hey, it's me, Jack. I need to ask a huge favor."

There was a long pause, and then Cindy cleared her throat.

Jack rolled his eyes and began again. "How are you, Cindy?"

"I'm fine, Jack. Thank you so much for asking. How can I help?"

Jack ran his fingers through his dripping wet hair. "I need you to run some background checks."

Jack ran down all the information he had on the three men named Terry.

"Got it." Cindy wrote so fast that he could hear her pen scratching. "How should I get it to you? Do you have email out in the sticks?"

"Yeah. I have my smartphone." Jack leaned closer to the wall and tucked his head down into his jacket. "Can you run one more? Alice Campbell."

"Alice? Our Alice?"

"Yes, Cindy, please?"

There was another long pause. "Jack, are you all right?"

The rough wooden shingles dug into the back of his hand as he pushed against the wall. "I'm good, Cindy." He stood up. "Thanks. I appreciate this." He hung up the phone.

The rain was a torrential downpour now. Visibility was only a few feet, but everything around him sparkled as the lights from the inn reflected off the drops that shattered against the porch. Jack could picture the old woman's face. He could still hear the breaking bowl and the glass chiming as it bounced along the floor.

She knew. I'm his son. My father was murdered. I had no control over that.

Jack looked up and stepped out. The rain ran down his upturned face, and he opened his eyes. He stared at the heavens and stood there, glaring up into the blackness.

I control the here and now—and now—it's my turn.

CHAPTER 13
Tea And A Bath

Jack walked back into the inn and stopped. As the water dripped off his face, he watched it fall onto a cranberry-red welcome mat.

"Mr. Stratton?" From behind the front counter, the innkeeper called to him. "Mr. Stratton, you're dripping on my floor."

He slowly lifted his chin and saw her disapproving gaze. She raised one eyebrow and folded her hands in front of her. The light-brown period dress she wore was different from the others. Those dresses all had high necklines, but this was cut low.

She reached behind the counter, grabbed two towels and hurried over to the door.

"Thank you." Jack took both towels and squatted down to wipe the floor. "My apologies."

"I can do that, Mr. Stratton." She reached for the towel but Jack mopped the floor with it.

"I made the mess, I can clean it up. You can call me Jack." He stood up and handed her the towel. The warmth of her fingers on his cold skin sent a glow racing down his wrist.

She inhaled sharply and slowly exhaled. The faint smell of chamomile reached him, and he grinned roguishly. Her eyes connected with his. "Can I get you anything else, Mr. Stratton?" The muscles around her eyes and mouth twitched slightly, revealing her struggle to keep a mask of refinement on her face.

Jack wiped the back of his neck with the other towel and waited a moment before he answered. "I've had a rough day. Do you have anything to drink?"

Her expression soured. "Mr. Stratton, there's a bar downtown—"

Jack leaned back and feigned a look of shock. His mind raced. "Ms. Jenkins, on a cold night like this, I was...only thinking of having a cup of tea to warm me."

She looked at him incredulously as he took a step back. "Tea? *You* wanted a cup of tea?"

Save. "I got caught in that downpour. Now I'm chilled to the bone. I thought I might go back to my room, get a good book, and relax in the bath with a nice cup of tea."

Her mouth plopped open.

Jack looked at her as innocently as a child. He was laying it on thick. Her head tilted slightly to the side, and her pursed lips relaxed and then slowly opened. Jack resisted the urge to smile as her eyes traveled over him while she appeared to be reappraising her opinion of him.

Jack handed her back the towel. "I'll have to remember to pick some up in town next time. I'm sorry to have troubled you, Ms. Jenkins."

Slump your shoulders. Small smile. Nod. Jack slowly moved for the staircase.

"Mr. Stratton, is there a particular brand of tea you prefer?"

Jack turned around with one foot on the stairs.

She walked forward, and her hands were now behind her back.

"Well, it sounds a little silly but on a rainy night like this, I just love a cup of chamomile tea."

Her eyebrows lifted, and her chest heaved.

Bang. Set the hook. Jack Stratton, you are so bad.

They both moved closer, and Jack could once again smell the flowers on her breath.

"Would you like me to bring some up?" she offered.

He gently touched her arm, nodded his head, and clamped his mouth shut, when he remembered—*Replacement's upstairs. Damn.*

"What's wrong?"

"My…" Jack coughed. "Coworker."

"That young woman isn't your girlfriend?" Disbelief and surprise, followed by understanding, flashed across her face.

Jack shrugged and nodded.

"That's why you wanted another room."

Game over. I shouldn't be flirting anyway. "Thanks anyhow." He sighed. Jack turned and started back up.

"Can I at least get you a cup to take back to your room?" she asked with a smile on her face that begged him to follow her. She never took her eyes off him as she backed around the counter toward the open door. Jack swallowed and forced himself to walk slowly after her. Her hand traced along the wood of the countertop. She was using it to guide herself as she walked backward, but the soft, feminine gesture sent a spark up Jack's spine.

Smiling, she turned and walked into the back room.

It was a dark interior room with only two tall lamp-stands for light. "I'll be right back. The water's already hot," she told him.

There was a door on each side, and she disappeared through the far one.

Jack frowned as he scanned the room. All the furniture was antique, as was the rug.

Damn. I'm still soaked.

Jack debated about running back upstairs and changing but drove that thought from his mind. He looked at the well-preserved chairs and couch and remained standing, slowly dripping on the carpet. He shivered, and the cold seemed to rush back into his being. His head fell forward; he leaned against the doorjamb and closed his eyes. The smell of the old house mixed with the scent of the rain was calming. He inhaled a couple of times and cleared his throat.

His eyes opened at the sound of the door clicking shut. Ms. Jenkins stood in the doorway with a tea tray in her left hand and a robe over her right arm.

Her eyes met his, and warmth spread inside his chest. Jack grinned and strode forward. He could see the flush on her neck as she swallowed.

"I thought you might need to warm up. I can dry your clothes." She set the tray on a small table beside the couch and walked over to him, both arms held out with the robe draped over them. "You can use that room to change." She tilted her head to the left but didn't take her eyes off Jack.

"Thank you." He took the robe and headed for the room on the right.

Slow down. Cool. Think about what you're doing...

It was a small bathroom with just a sink, a toilet, and an ornate, full-length mirror stand. Jack's hands shook as he quickly removed his clothes. He couldn't tell whether it was the cold or nervousness.

How old is she? Mid-forties? She doesn't look it. Dancer? Guaranteed she's a dancer.

The robe could have been custom-made for him. It was a dark blue with ornate trim and fabric, matching the historical feel of the house. If you could travel back in time one hundred years, everything would look just like this. It was soft and warm, as if she'd just taken it out of the dryer. Jack relaxed into the warmth and closed his eyes. When he reopened them, he straightened up, checked himself in the mirror, and stood even taller. The robe gave him a regal appearance. He spoke into the mirror. "Lord Jack of Tingsberry."

He opened the door and the woman was posed at the end of the couch. Jack paused.

She smiled and held out a cup. "Tea?"

Jack sat down at the edge of the couch and took the ornate teacup with a widening smile. "Thank you..." He let his words hang in the air as he realized he didn't know her name.

"Kristine," she answered with a slight nod.

A small moan escaped Jack's lips as he sipped the tea. "That's really good tea," he said, surprised. He wasn't a tea man at all.

Kristine smiled broadly, set her cup down, and folded her hands in her lap. "Tea and a bath..." She tilted her head. "Do you really like to take baths?"

Jack thought for a moment about protesting to continue the charade, but one look at her face caused him to dismiss the idea.

She's smart. She'll see right through it.

"You're right. I haven't taken a bath since I was seven." He smiled.

"Which probably wasn't that long ago."

Jack saw his chance for romance plummeting. In situations like this, he went to his old standby: he told the truth.

"Kristine, I wasn't interested in a bath or tea. Honestly, at first, I wanted to tease you a little for not giving me a room refund, but..." he exhaled and looked into her eyes, "there was also something about you. The way you move, like a dancer. When I got close to you, I could feel your breath and I smelled the chamomile."

"Oh. I thought that part was too good to be true. You're a good detective. What do you do for a living?"

Jack lifted his chin. "I'm a cop."

"Figures." She leaned in. "I was a dancer."

Jack leaned in, too, but was taken aback when in one swift move she kissed him.

Think about what you're doing. I shouldn't. I shouldn't...I should.

With one hand, Jack lifted her up slightly off the couch and pulled her forward enough to be reclining. The move was so fast and fluid that Kristine exhaled as he gently laid her down. Jack's eyes closed as he let the different sensations wash over him: the softness of her hair in his left hand and the firmness of her toned back in his right. Chamomile faintly danced on his tongue. Her hands drew him closer, and his leg rubbed against hers.

He slowly lowered his body onto hers, opened his eyes, and smiled back as she searched his face. Long lashes led to blue eyes that widened as he moved his hand down her side.

"That was some kiss," she whispered and leaned forward again.

"You're a good teacher."

Her face went white. She blinked slowly as she looked up at him.

Jack leaned in, but all the warmth from her lips was gone.

She pressed her lips together as her body went rigid. "Get out." She kept her eyes closed.

Jack froze. "I'm sorry. Did I..." he stammered.

"Just leave, please."

This was the age of "no means no," but he couldn't understand the one-eighty turnaround.

"Are you all right?"

"Now." She clenched her jaw. She kept her eyes closed as she turned her head away from him and toward the back of the couch.

Jack carefully lifted himself off her and backed up toward the door. He moved quietly and quickly but hesitated when he grabbed the old doorknob.

"I'm sorry if..." His words trailed off.

Kristine pulled her legs up and curled into a ball. He opened the door just enough to slip through and closed it behind him.

Damn it! My clothes.

Jack stood behind the desk in the ornate robe. Shoes, pants, and, most importantly, his keys were in the bathroom. He debated with himself for only a moment before he headed up the stairs.

This blows. This is so bad.

He pulled the robe tighter around himself as the young couple from yesterday's breakfast walked past him. They gave him an odd look, and he could hear them giggle as he passed.

Damn.

CHAPTER 14
Complimentary Laundry

The door handle to his room turned and opened. He breathed a sigh of relief. If this had been a normal hotel, he would have been trapped in the hallway, but Replacement hadn't locked the door.

"What happened to you?" Replacement snickered as he walked into the room. She sat up in bed, wrapped in a fluffy robe of her own, but her smile quickly vanished. "Where did you get that robe?"

"Um…my clothes were wet. The…front desk offered…to do the complimentary laundry."

"They do laundry?" Her neck lengthened, and her nose crinkled.

"Yeah. So they gave me a robe."

"Can they dry my stuff?" She slid out of bed.

"No, they…only do one load per room a day. I'm sorry…I didn't think."

"It's okay." Her shoulders popped up and down. "I hung mine up in the bathroom. Do you want to take a bath?"

Jack shook his head.

Bath and a cup a tea? I'd have liked Kristine in the bath but… Why do I get the psycho ones?

"Are you going to sleep with me tonight?" Replacement asked innocently.

Jack's head snapped up at the question, and his neck flushed. Replacement's expression didn't change as she continued to wait for him to answer her question regarding sleep and sleep only.

He sighed. "No. Thank you."

"Please sleep with me." She scooted around onto her knees in a mock begging position.

Jack swallowed. "I have…my air mattress." He grabbed the box and held it up, turning away quickly.

"Suit yourself." Replacement threw her hands in the air and fell back on the bed.

After forty-five minutes of huffing and puffing, the mattress was only half-filled with air. Jack leaned back against the bureau, and Replacement slid off the bed.

"Finally. My turn." She picked up the corner of the mattress and began to blow air into it. Jack watched her for a few moments, and his eyes rolled up to the ceiling. A debate raged inside him now. On one hand: Replacement was Chandler's sister and a guy took care of his best friend's kid sister. On the other hand…

She said it herself…she doesn't even consider me to be a big brother. She's right: I wasn't at Aunt Haddie's while she was there. She likes me, and

I—Stop it, Jack. I'm just worked up because of Kristine, and I haven't had a date in...

"See?" Replacement hit his leg. "See how good I am? I'm way better at blowing than you. I only did it for a few minutes, and it's almost all the way up." She inhaled deeply and then breathed into the valve again. Jack shifted his position and held out his hands.

"Okay. That's good enough."

Replacement stopped, put down the mattress, and leaned onto it. It made a creaking sound as she bounced.

"I can sleep here," she offered. "This is bouncy." She got up on the mattress on all fours and bounced up and down. The bouncing was loosening her robe and it was slowly opening. He sat up a little straighter as the robe released a little more.

Just a couple more bounces...

Jack sighed and held up his hand to cover the view offered as her robe neared the fully opening point. Replacement saw what he was doing and awkwardly scurried off the mattress, clutching her robe together.

"That's good. Thank you. I'll sleep here." Jack grabbed a sheet and blanket and moved onto the rubber contraption.

Replacement hurried back and wrapped herself in blankets. "Okay. Night."

Jack lay sleepless as he tried to force himself to remain absolutely motionless. The slightest movement caused the whole bed to wobble like Jell-O. Morbid and dark thoughts slammed into his head, and now he felt helpless to even move. Depression washed over him.

Make a list for tomorrow. Get the info from Cindy. One by one, talk to the three suspects. What the hell happened with Kristine? Did she...maybe she just changed her mind. I didn't see a ring. No indentation. What about...?

A slight hissing sound started at the top of the mattress. It quickly changed to a noise like a kid's whoopee cushion, and then stopped. Jack kept his eyes closed and rolled his head in the direction of the noise. The movement alone was enough to cause another noise, as if someone farted, and it lasted for a few seconds this time.

Damn it.

Jack waited. The sound stopped. He listened for several more moments and rolled his head back to look up at the ceiling. Another long farty noise started, but this time it kept going.

Replacement giggled. After another few seconds, he did, too. Soon they both were crying with laughter as his bed slowly deflated.

Jack stopped laughing when his body finally settled onto the hard floor. He stood up, grabbed his blanket and lay down near the door. He lay on his back and stared at the ceiling. Sleep wouldn't come. Every time he shut his eyes, he could see those faces. His mother's face would change back and forth between her young self and the woman screaming at the institution.

Silently screaming is how he pictured his mother, her finger outstretched, terror in her eyes. Now three more faces tormented him.

The old woman from the store was really his grandmother. He could see the tears roll down her cheeks and her trembling lips.

She touched me. I'm her grandson. Will she believe it? Will she care?

Steven's face flashed before him, but it was unclear. He couldn't bring it up in his mind clearly. Jack thought about grabbing the yearbook and looking again but stopped himself.

He was just a kid. Seventeen.

Jack rolled over, and now Kristine's face haunted him too.

Why? Why did she freak out? Now I'm stuck here for another five days, or I eat that money but—

Just outside the door, someone placed something down. Jack silently drew his legs up, rolled over, and crouched. He hadn't heard the footsteps approach, but he did hear them leaving. His hand hesitated on the doorknob for only a moment before he cracked the door open. Next to the door were his clothes, neatly folded in a pile with his shoes on top. He was tempted to sprint down the stairs after her, but instead quietly picked up his clothes and retreated into the room.

CHAPTER 15

The Foreman

The next morning, Jack read over the reports Cindy had sent him. Jack flipped back to the first Terry on the list; Replacement rushed out of the bathroom. She wore her new "I Love Hope Falls" shirt and hat.

She stopped short. "You look like crap."

"Thanks. Are you ready?" Jack wanted to get moving and avoid Kristine. He didn't know what kind of scene awaited him downstairs.

He looked into the mirror in the bathroom and he had to admit that Replacement was right: he looked like hell. His skin was pale and there were dark circles under his eyes. He walked toward the mirror as he looked at his reflection. Even his pupils seemed black.

"Let's go." He spun around and stormed out of the room. Replacement chased after him.

"What's the first stop?" She had to jog to stay beside him.

"Terry Bradford. He's a foreman at K and K Construction. It's a ten-minute drive."

"How did you find that out?"

"Cindy got me his information. Guy has bounced from one low-level job to another. One DUI. Married three times. Divorced. Four kids by three different mothers. Two bankruptcies."

"Boy, he's a keeper. Do you want me to drive?"

Jack shot her a crooked frown so she headed for the passenger side.

"Do you have a plan?" she asked hopefully.

Jack jumped in the car, grateful he hadn't seen Kristine. He started the engine and sped out of the little parking lot.

"9:04. Construction workers should all be there by now."

"Do you have a plan?

"No. I'll play it by ear."

Replacement raised her eyebrows. "Well…shouldn't we come up with a plan first?"

"Yes. Don't scream. Don't yell. As I calmly ask him if he had anything to do with murdering my father, and if he gives me a sideways glance, I'm going to beat him to death."

"That sounds like a great plan." Replacement's lip curled.

Jack punched it.

As they headed through downtown, Jack noticed an old white pickup weaving through traffic behind them. He pulled down the rearview mirror.

"Is everything okay?" Replacement craned her neck to look behind them.

Jack slowed down.

The pickup took a sharp right from the left lane. They passed a building that blocked their view of the truck as it drove down the side road.

"I'm just paranoid." Jack positioned the rearview mirror back.

The Impala slid into the parking lot at K and K Construction. The mini-mountains of gravel, sand, and stone behind the structure dwarfed the building. Giant machines loaded large trucks while a group of men gathered out front.

Jack parked and opened the door. A couple of men who were loading a pickup truck stopped and turned to watch Jack as he stalked up.

"I'm looking for Terry Bradford?" Jack asked.

The men just looked at each other and then back at Jack.

"Just point me in the right direction," Jack grumbled.

They looked at each other again. As a cop, Jack had seen the look a thousand times.

No one wants to be a snitch.

Replacement tapped Jack's shoulder and tilted her head toward the building. A group of five men in green shirts, jeans, and work boots marched out of the office. Jack zeroed in on the guy in the middle.

Early forties. Five ten. Two hundred pounds.

Terry Bradford was twenty-six years older than the yearbook photo and apparently shaved his head now, but Jack knew it was him.

Jack jogged over. "Terry, you got a second?"

Four of them stopped.

Terry kept walking.

"I just have a few questions." Jack forced a smile onto his face.

"I'm workin'. Talk to me later." Terry held up a hand.

"It'll only take a second." Jack walked in front of him. "I need to ask you about Steven Ritter?"

"Who? I don't know any Ritter. Get the hell out of my way, or I'll break your nose." He stopped and made a face as if he drank extra-sour lemonade. "Who?"

"Steven Ritter. You went to high school with him."

"Ritter? Was that the kid who got killed at the pond?"

"Yes."

"I didn't know him. He was a year under me. He didn't play football, right?"

Jack shook his head.

"Then I didn't know him. We gotta be someplace," Terry snapped before he stepped forward and got right in Jack's face. "Move."

They stood nose to nose and glared at each other. "Did you know Patricia Cole?"

Terry made a face again. "Patty? Put-out Patty?" His tongue hung out of his open mouth as he laughed. "Everyone knew Patty…if you know what I mean."

Jack's hand twitched into a fist, and Replacement put her hand on his arm.

"You guys on vacation?" a large man bellowed from the building's doorway. "Get your asses in gear, now!"

Replacement kept her hand on Jack's arm, while Terry walked around him and got behind the wheel of the truck. The veins in Jack's neck stood out.

"Not now," she whispered. "Get him alone."

As the truck pulled out of the parking lot, Terry roared with laughter and pounded the side of the door as he ripped out.

Jack turned and stormed back for the Impala. Replacement dashed over to it and stood in front of his door.

"Out of my way."

"Not now, Jack." She put both hands on the door handle. "You taught me that. Wait until you can ask him alone. You know where he lives, right?"

"He could be the guy who killed my father."

"He could, or he might not be."

Jack glared at the sky. *Damn it. I'm too close to this. I can't think straight.* He looked back down at Replacement and nodded.

"We'll go back at him tonight," Replacement said. "When he's alone."

"I'll get him to talk to me then."

Replacement didn't move. "What are you doing? You went straight at Terry. We can't do that with this next guy. You know what to do. What questions to ask. You're a policeman."

"Not out here. Not right now."

Replacement squared her shoulders. "Yes, right now. You're always a cop." She pointed at his heart. "But you need to be one here too." She tapped her temple. "After all, when we do find the guy, and we will, we need to get evidence that we can take to the police, not kill the guy." She smiled.

Jack didn't.

"We're going to take the evidence we get to the police, right?"

Jack didn't answer her. He opened his door. "Let's go talk to Terry Martin."

CHAPTER 16

The Fiduciary

They parked outside the small, modern, two-story office building. The parking lot was three-quarters filled with over a dozen cars. All of them looked as though they'd just come off the dealership lot. Jack scanned the large brass mailbox next to the entrance. A number of names were etched into the plates.

Different companies must rent the space.

"Two oh six. Second floor," he snapped as he held open the door.

Replacement turned, looked up at him, and flashed a big smile. "How about letting me do the talking on this one?"

"I said keep me in check, not on a leash." Jack looked down at her. "I'll do the talking. Just make sure I don't flip out."

"How am I going to do that? Can I have a gun?" She grinned.

"No." He winced. "Is that your plan to stop me? Shoot me?"

"I wasn't thinking that, but since you suggested it…" Her hands went out and she grinned impishly. "I just don't want *you* shooting anyone."

"I'm not going to shoot anyone. I wouldn't use a gun to kill him, anyway."

"That's reassuring."

The building had a simple layout with offices at the center. The marble floor and the gleaming metal with glass accents shined in the sunlight.

"The tenants must pay a lot for rent here," Replacement noted.

As they walked into the building, Jack went cold thinking about what he would do when he did find the guy who killed his father. He forced himself to keep moving and took the stairs two at a time. The staircase opened into another floor of offices. They continued to walk until they saw a large oak door with a bronze sign: Terry Martin—Fiduciary Advisor.

Replacement pointed at "Fiduciary" and raised an eyebrow.

"This is the one who looked like a weasel," Jack spat.

"That might not be the best way to start."

Jack opened the door. An elegant oak desk was near the far wall, with a closed oak door to the right of it. Four leather chairs stood against the left wall. A glass coffee table with a neat stack of magazines was just in front of them. Two chairs were in the corner on the right with a little table and more magazines between those. The room was empty.

Jack and Replacement exchanged a shrug as they walked in. Jack moved over to the secretary's desk. The computer was on, and there was a cup of coffee next to the keyboard. Replacement cleared her throat as she nodded her head toward the closed door. She raised her eyebrows twice and grinned.

Jack walked over to the door to listen. He could hear the sound of lovemaking behind the door.

Replacement made a disgusted face. "Maybe we should go," she whispered.

Jack rapped hard on the door.

"Or not." Replacement moved back.

A minute later, the door opened and a young, disheveled, blonde-haired secretary stood wide-eyed before them, smiling awkwardly.

"Who is it?" A man's voice inside called out.

Jack walked past her and through the door.

A tall, middle-aged man adjusted his clothes as he moved behind his desk. Terry Martin had a large nose, pockmarked face, and dyed hair that he combed over.

"Do you have an appointment?" he snapped as he sat down and continued to adjust his clothes.

"My name is Jack Stratton." Jack strode over to the two chairs in front of the desk and sat down. He didn't offer the man his hand. "I just have a few questions for you."

"Are you looking for financial advice?"

"Did you know Patricia Cole?" Jack asked.

"Subtle," Replacement whispered as she slid into the seat next to him.

"What?" Terry swiveled in his high-back chair. "Cole? I knew a Patty Cole, but that was in high school."

"How did you know Patty?"

"What? Who are you?"

"Did you know Patty? Did you date her?"

"Date her? You didn't 'date' Patty. We, uh…I was—did my wife send you?" Terry leaned forward. "That hag. She can't get anything on me, so she goes back to some slut I screwed in high school?"

Jack's knuckles went white on the chair. The muscles in his jaw flexed, and Replacement shifted in her seat. Terry jumped up, and so did Replacement.

She held up her hands. "We don't know your wife. We're doing some historic research and we're hoping you could please—"

Terry stormed around the desk, grabbed her by the arm and yanked her toward the door. "Get the hell out—"

"Let go of her." Jack flew out of his chair.

Terry let go, stumbled backward and fell into the wall. As he slumped to the floor, a picture crashed to the ground and the glass cracked.

"You piece of garbage." Jack stepped toward him.

"Jack." Replacement held Jack's arm.

"Terry!" The office door flew open, and the secretary rushed into the room. "Leave him alone." She rushed toward Jack, but Replacement stepped between them.

"Your boyfriend fell." Replacement's feet were wide and her shoulders were square as she blocked her.

"What about Steven? Steven Ritter?" Jack towered over Terry.

"Steven? Steve?" Terry didn't even try to get up. "The one who was murdered at the pond?"

"Did you know him?"

"He was in some of my classes. I knew him since we were kids. Why? What does this have to do with my wife?"

"I don't know your wife. Get up," Jack ordered.

Terry froze. "I don't know anything about Steven getting killed. Did someone say I did? That's crazy."

"I'm calling the cops," the secretary said.

Replacement shook her head. "There's no need to do that. We were just leaving."

"He knew Steven." Jack turned back to Terry. "I said get up."

Terry rose but kept his hands out in front of himself as if he were facing a wild dog. "I liked Steve. I had nothing to do with it. I couldn't stab someone. I've never even been in a fight. I can't fight my way out of a paper bag. Honest. I don't know why anyone would say... Wait. Was it Patty? Is she still mad at me? If Patty said I had anything to do with it, she's just out for revenge."

"Revenge for what?" Jack asked.

"She wanted to join the band. I told her I could get her in. It was just a con. I really just wanted to get in her pants, but that was a long time ago."

"You used her." Jack stepped forward and the picture on the floor crunched beneath his heel.

"I was in high school. Guys did that crap."

"Looks like you haven't learned your lesson." Replacement tilted her head toward the secretary, who was now fuming.

Terry hurried behind his desk. "I'm calling the police." He reached for the phone.

Replacement jerked her thumb at the secretary, whose disgusted glare was withering. "Right now, Terry, I'd be more worried she's going to call your wife."

Terry straightened up and combed back his hair. "Get out now."

Jack spoke in a low voice. "Here's the deal. I don't care who the hell you call. I want to know where you were the night Steven was killed." Jack put his hand on the desk.

Terry's eyes widened. "Wait a second... Are you... You're Steven's son."

Jack walked around the desk.

"Wait! I can prove I had nothing to do with it. Spain!" He shouted the word. "The whole AP Spanish class went. I remember. I had to call my mom to find out who got killed. The teacher only told us someone from school died. There's got to be a record of the trip and who was on it."

Jack's head pounded. He glared at Terry, who took another step back.

"I liked Steven. I did. Check. Check with the school."

"I will." Jack spun on his heels and headed for the door.

As Jack passed the secretary, she glared at Terry and said, "Helping me get by the CPA exam—was that just a lie to get in my pants, too?"

Jack stormed out of the building. Getting to the car and leaving was a blur. His anger boiled over. He had no clue where he was going; he was just driving.

"Jack? Jack, pull over," Replacement urged him. He kept driving. "Pull over." Replacement put her hand on the door handle, feigning she was about to open it. "Now."

Jack knew she was serious. He hit the brake and pulled over.

"Jack…"

He opened the door and jumped out of the car. She did, too.

"What the hell were you thinking, Jack?"

"What was I thinking?" Jack spun around. "I wasn't thinking at all." He could see the shocked look on her face as she stared at him. He could only imagine how he looked. "I wanted to beat him to death. I didn't just want to hurt him; I wanted him dead. Okay? Is that what you want to hear? I'm not thinking straight." Jack's eyes were black, and his hands shook.

"Jack, I don't think he had anything to do with it."

"I know, but right now I don't care." He kicked a rock off the road and into the woods. "I just… Damn it. It's not just Steven. It's Patty too. I don't know why, but I keep thinking of Patty as a kid. She just wanted to get into the band, and he used her. I should have done something."

She crossed her arms over her chest. "Maybe we should leave for now. You're losing all perspective."

"I'm not going anywhere. Someone killed my father. I have to find out who." Jack glared up at the gray sky and wanted to scream.

"Jack, you're going to do something you're seriously going to regret if you don't keep your anger in check. There are three guys named Terry."

"We still have to go talk to the other one," Jack informed her.

"What?" Replacement threw her hands up. "You just…do you think talking to the other guy is at all wise? So far, your plan is to yell and accuse. You're not even asking questions. That guy has an alibi that we can check out. You're just screaming. That's just stupid."

"One of them did it. I just need to figure out which one."

"Not with me. I'm having nothing more to do with your professional suicide."

"Fine. You talk." Jack looked down at his hands. His head pounded.

She didn't move.

He hung his head and tried to slow his breathing. He cracked his neck as he looked back at her. "Please?"

Replacement put her hands on her hips and shook her head. She searched his eyes, and then exhaled. "I'll do it, but you have to agree to three things. First, I do all the talking." She held up a hand. "All the talking."

"Fine."

"Second, I drive." She held out a hand, and he tossed her the keys.

"Third, you sleep in the stupid bed tonight."

Jack hesitated, but then said, "Agreed."

As Replacement stood there, her face softened. "Jack, I'm worried about you."

"Don't be." Jack walked to the passenger side of the car. "I got you watching my back. What could go wrong?"

CHAPTER 17

Nothing to Worry About

Jack sat in the passenger seat and watched in the side view mirror as a police car drove behind them. "Cop," he muttered.

"I see him." Replacement smiled as she held her hands at a perfect ten and two position on the steering wheel. She stopped at the stop sign and put her blinker on. "Besides, we have nothing to worry about as long as we obey the speed limits and since I'm driving——"

Blue lights flashed and a siren kicked on.

"You were saying?" Jack said.

"What the heck?" Replacement pulled over. "I didn't do anything wrong."

"I bet Terry Martin called the cops." Jack sat up straighter. "I knew I should have put him through the wall."

"That would have been a big help." Replacement made a face as she got her license out.

After a minute, a policeman with a crisp white shirt and salt-and-pepper hair marched over to Replacement's window. "License and registration."

She handed him her license and registration. "What seems to be the problem, Officer?" she asked innocently.

The policeman took the paperwork and headed back to the cruiser without saying a word.

"That was rude," Replacement muttered.

"He's a lieutenant." Jack watched him in the side view mirror. "The town's so small they must have everyone pulling patrol."

"But I didn't do anything. Do you think Terry called?"

Jack shook his head. "No. He didn't ask for my license or even look at me."

They both kept watching until the policeman came back and held out a ticket.

"What?" Replacement's voice went high as she read the ticket. "Failure to yield at an intersection?"

"She came to a full stop," Jack protested.

"You can contest it." The policeman's voice was flat.

One look at the man's set jaw and unsympathetic expression and Jack knew that arguing was most likely pointless but he still had to try. He read the nametag as he leaned forward.

"Lieutenant Nelson, sir, I can assure you that she did come to a complete——"

"You can explain it at traffic court." Nelson straightened up and folded his hands in front of himself. "Your girlfriend needs to obey the law. Have a nice day." He turned and started back for his car.

Jack bristled. "What a jerk."

Replacement started the Impala.

The flashing blue lights shut off behind them. Jack tried unsuccessfully not to glare as Nelson pulled out and drove away.

"Maybe we should just go back to the hotel," Replacement suggested. "Then you can get some sleep."

"No. I agreed to your terms. We go talk to Terry Martinez first."

CHAPTER 18
The Art Teacher

Replacement parked the car in front of the modest Cape Cod-style house. Painted a deep red with black shutters, it fit right in with the other four homes on the beautiful cul-de-sac. A group of children rode bikes down the sidewalk. A cinnamon-brown sedan was parked in the driveway.

"Okay," Replacement breathed out. "Terry Martinez. He's a teacher?"

"High school art. Widower. Wife died five years ago. No arrests. Finances in order."

"I do all the talking, right?" Replacement leaned in.

Jack moved his fingers in a horizontal zipping motion across his mouth.

As they got out of the car, a middle-aged man opened the front door and walked outside. His black hair was tinted gray at the sides. He was short and his blue T-shirt revealed a bit of a paunch. He tipped his head to the side, stopped halfway down the steps, and then waited for them to approach.

"Terry Martinez?" Replacement smiled as she held out her hand. "I'm Alice Campbell. This is Jack Stratton."

Replacement's nose crinkled as she said her own name, but it was the look Terry gave him that caught Jack's attention. Terry's eyes traveled around Jack's face like someone would examine a painting. Terry's eyes moved to look at his mouth, nose, chin, and finally his eyes. Jack held out his hand, and Terry hesitated for a moment before he shook it firmly.

"How can I help you?" Terry's mouth curled up at the corner.

"I was wondering if we could speak with you about some people you went to high school with?"

"High school." He smiled and adjusted his glasses. "That was a long time ago, but I'd be happy to. Uh...do you want to come in?"

"That's very kind of you." Replacement nodded.

Terry turned around and went back in the house; they followed. Inside was not at all what Jack had expected from an art teacher's home. It was a very neat and tidy, conservative house. The front door opened to a staircase, a dining room to the left, and a traditional living room on the right.

Terry motioned them to a small couch. "Can I get you something to drink?"

"No, thank you," Replacement answered and Jack shook his head no.

Terry moved over to sit in a worn but comfortable-looking blue chair.

"How can I help you?" He put his hands on his thighs and leaned forward.

"We were wondering if you knew a Patricia Cole?" Replacement folded her hands on her lap.

Terry leaned back, frowned, and nodded his head. "Patty. I knew her. She grew up over on Winston. No brothers or sisters."

"Can you tell us a little about her?"

Terry took his glasses off and cleaned them on his shirt. "What's this all about?"

"We're doing some family research, and it would be very helpful if you could fill in some information we need."

Terry's eyes went wide; he leaned in to stare at Jack. He tilted his head and pursed his lips. "I never thought…Patty is your mother."

"How did you know?" Jack asked, surprised.

Terry smiled and patted the arm of his chair. "The resemblance. I'm an artist. I've got a thing for faces. I knew you must be Steve's son—"

Replacement gasped. Terry looked nervously at both of them.

Terry blurted, "You knew that, right?"

"Yes." Jack nodded. "And I look a little like him."

"A little? Not identical, but almost. The whole shape of your face. The eyes are spot-on. Indistinguishable." He clucked his tongue and held up a hand. "One second."

Terry hurried out of the room and returned a moment later carrying a framed photo. "Here."

Jack took the frame, and Replacement slid closer. Four boys in shorts held up fishing poles with a tiny fish at the end. They were all smiling. Steven was in the middle. He must have been in his early teens.

Replacement pointed. "He looks just like you."

Terry sat back down and sniffed. "I'm so sorry about Steven. You couldn't have known him, right?"

Jack shook his head. "I didn't even know his name before this week."

"Is this you?" Replacement pointed to a boy in the photo.

"Sure is. I was chubbier then."

Jack looked back at the fat kid in the photo with the curly black hair and a giant smile.

"Were you friends?" Replacement asked.

"The four of us were best friends. Same Boy Scout troop. We all knew each other since preschool."

"Who are the other boys?"

"Trent Dorsey and Dennis Wilson. Trent passed ten years ago. Car accident in Baltimore."

"And Dennis?"

"He's the police chief. He lives on Davidson. Big gray colonial."

Jack held up a hand. "Dennis Wilson? Dennis Wilson was chief when Steven died. How *old* is he?"

"That was Dennis Senior. He was the chief then. His son became chief maybe twelve years ago."

Steven's friend is now chief. I've a much better shot at the police reports now.

Terry frowned as he looked at Jack. "Steven was a good guy. I don't know if anyone...Mrs. Ritter. Jack..." Terry's eyes filled with concern. "Steven's mother still lives in town."

Replacement leaned in. "We're going to speak with her later. You knew Patty?"

"I did. It's a small town, so everyone knows everybody. She was in my class. We went to high school together."

Replacements voice softened. "Did you ever...date Patty?"

"Date? No. I had a huge crush on her in middle school. I wouldn't go near her then because of her father. Mr. Cole's as mean as they come. He's a drinker, too. I thought about it in high school, but she'd gotten a...well." Terry started to clean his glasses again, but this time he didn't look up.

Jack broke the awkward silence. "I've heard. She had a reputation."

Terry exhaled. "In high school, she did. Something changed in her in middle school. It was after her mom died. Maybe it was that. Maybe it was her father. I don't know. She just seemed to fly apart. I didn't know Steven dated her."

"You didn't know they dated?" Replacement stared at the photo.

"No. But...boy, just thinking about it. On one hand, it was twenty-something years ago, but on the other it feels like yesterday." Terry smiled sadly. "Steve was getting over a bad breakup before he was killed. I didn't think he started dating again." Terry smiled sideways at Jack. "I was always jealous of your dad."

Jack nodded.

"Steve was such a good kid. He was a Boy Scout. Back then, Patty's reputation wasn't that good. Steve wasn't the type of guy to go with—"

Jack finished the sentence. "A girl like that?"

Terry nodded and continued. "I came back for the funeral—"

"Came back?" Jack asked.

"My parents divorced at the start of my senior year. My dad stayed in Hope Falls, but I'd moved to Cincinnati with my mom."

"You weren't living here when he was killed?"

"No. I was living in Ohio then." The teacher's eyes went wide, and he sat back. "Wait a minute. Are you looking into it? Me? Why would you think I had anything to do with it?" His voice got higher.

"Settle down." Jack stood. "I don't think you had anything to do with it."

"I didn't. Steve was my friend."

"I believe you." Jack sighed.

"I don't," Replacement mumbled but they both could hear her.

"What?" Terry held up his hands.

"Well..." She shrugged. "I don't know. You show us a picture and act all nice but it could be an act."

"Why would you think I had anything to do with it? I wasn't even in the state."

"We got a tip," Jack snapped.

"A tip to look at me? I don't believe you." Terry stood up straighter.

"They weren't specific. They only had a first name: Terry." Jack ran his hands through his hair. "Thank you for your time."

"I'm sorry. Wait." Terry moved closer to the door. "There are other guys named Terry. Terry Martin. He was a pain in the ass at school. Martin and Martinez? People always got us confused. They could have meant him?"

"I talked to him already."

"Did he say anything?" Terry paced. "There was also a Terry in the grade above us. Football player. He was a jerk."

"Talked to him, too. Thank you." Jack headed for the door.

"Would it be possible to talk to you again, please?" Replacement glared at Jack.

"Sure. Jack, if I said anything to offend you, I'm sorry. If you need anything, please let me help."

"Thank you." Jack stomped down the steps to the car, and Replacement hurried after him.

"What the hell was that? Why are we leaving?" She grabbed his shoulder, but he was too strong for her to turn him around, so he just stopped.

"What? I didn't do anything, and now you're pissed? I didn't hit him."

"He's the first person who would talk to us. He knew both your parents."

"Don't call them that," Jack snapped.

"He knew them both. He might know something that will help."

"He just gave us an alibi we can check out. We back off for now and let him sweat. Just because his mother moved to Cincinnati doesn't mean he didn't come back to visit his father for a weekend. I plan at going back at him later, but not now. I've held up two out of three of your stupid rules. I want to go back to the inn and sleep."

Replacement nodded. "Okay. You can get a good night's sleep, and tomorrow will be a new day, right?"

If I make it to tomorrow.

CHAPTER 19

Drown It

Jack splashed water on his face and reached for the towel.

Terry. Terry who? She gets him killed and she can't even tell me the last name of the guy who killed him?

After he dried his face, he looked in the mirror, and the towel fell out of his hands. He stared at his reflection and barely recognized himself: pale and gaunt, with brown eyes set deep in his skull.

I have to get some sleep. I look like death.

Jack walked out of the bathroom and stopped in his tracks. Replacement had his phone in her hands and looked as if she wanted to kill him.

"What? I'm following your stupid rule, and I want to go to sleep."

She held the phone up.

"I went to look at the report for Terry Bradford and saw this. You asked Cindy to run a background check on me?"

Jack froze.

Damn.

He shook his head. "No. We got in that fight about not knowing each other, so I wanted to find out more about you."

"So you had Cindy run a background check?"

"How else was I going to find out more about you?"

"How about asking? You could have…you should…" Replacement ran into the bathroom, and slammed the door.

Damn.

Jack's fist came down on the bureau, and something cracked. He stormed over to the closet and yanked the door open. He locked his gun in the safe, grabbed his wallet and keys and headed out the door. He stomped down the stairs, out the front door, and straight to his car.

Jack drummed his fingers on the steering wheel as he fought to drive out the thoughts that assaulted him. It didn't work. Rage seethed inside him. Pain. Hurt. It was useless to fight it now.

The only way I know to kill the pain—drown it.

The drive to the bar was short. It was a hole-in-the-wall, single-room bar on a side road. Several cars and trucks were parked outside. Jack went straight through the door and paused for a second as his eyes adjusted to the dimly lit room.

He smiled.

My kind of bar.

There was one long bar with stools in front and four small tables along the wall. A man in his sixties with pale skin, yellowed teeth, and dull, black eyes stood behind the bar. Of the seven guys in the room, three looked at him but only for a moment. Jack headed to the far stool against the wall.

"Whiskey. Neat." Jack slapped a handful of bills down.

The glass barely touched the wood before he downed it in one swallow. "Again."

He repeated the process two more times before he paused. The bartender hurried to the other end of the bar. Jack swirled his drink and smiled wryly.

I'll sleep tonight.

No one came near him at the end of the bar. Jack kept throwing bills down, but his glass stayed full only momentarily. He didn't talk. He didn't look up. He just drank.

An hour later, Jack was ready to go. He licked his lips and closed one eye as he tried to figure out how many bills to leave. In the end, he let a few fall from his hands and stuffed the others in his pocket. The door at the front of the bar opened, and three men with green shirts and work boots walked through. Terry Bradford came in last.

It took Jack two tries to stand. One of the men looked at Jack and tapped Terry on the arm.

"Hey," Terry called out. "Lookie who's here. You lookin' for me?"

Jack grinned.

The perfect end to this day.

"Yeah." Jack walked forward. "I've got something to ask. You said something about Patty."

"Pump-me Patty? Yeah." He laughed and nudged the guy next to him. "I bet a lot of guys can tell you about her. You want details? How she—"

That was all Jack could take. Jack's fist flashed out and drove straight into Terry's face.

Terry staggered back.

Jack grabbed him and heaved him out the door. Barstools overturned, and men rushed to get out of the way. Someone tackled Jack from behind, and both of them tumbled outside. Terry had already started to get to his feet.

Jack hit the guy who'd tackled him in the groin. The man coughed and rolled onto his back. The other guy, who'd come in with Terry, stood in the doorway but didn't come outside. Jack struggled to his feet and wobbled in a half circle. Terry stood there, holding his nose.

Jack took two steps forward.

Terry pulled his hand down and snarled, "You piece of—"

The second punch caught Terry on the chin. His mouth closed with a pop, but he remained on his feet. Jack hit him again. His head snapped back, and this time he fell to his knees. Jack swayed and staggered. He grabbed Terry by the collar to gain his balance.

"Patty is my mother," Jack snarled and hit him again. "Steven Ritter's my father." He hit him again. "Steven Ritter. Remember him now? Did you kill my father?"

"FREEZE!"

Jack looked up, and a young cop in his early twenties stood, shaking, before him. The lights from his cruiser made Jack blink, and the police siren hurt his ears.

"Am I that loud when I show up?"

Terry knelt on the ground while Jack held him up by his collar. Jack let go and Terry fell backward. Jack staggered but remained on his feet.

"Hands up. Put your hands up," the cop ordered, but his voice trembled. Jack held up his arms and slowly stumbled back.

"Move away from…that guy."

Terry groaned.

Jack smiled and lowered his arms.

"Keep your hands up." The cop's voice went high.

"I need to put my arms down." Jack shook his head. "I'm too drunk to keep 'em up."

More sirens blared as a second cruiser flew into the parking lot and stopped in a cloud of dust. Nelson, the policeman who pulled him over earlier in the day, got out. The wrinkles on his lined face deepened as he marched over.

"You again," Nelson growled.

"Hi." Jack waved.

The old cop grimaced. "Put some cuffs on him, Kenny, while I check on Terry."

"Yes, sir," Kenny replied.

Terry sat up as Nelson walked over to him.

Kenny pulled Jack over to his police cruiser, and turned him around. Jack relaxed against the cruiser and put his head down on the roof.

"Do you have any weapons on you?" The young policeman patted Jack down.

"Nope," Jack muttered.

Kenny grabbed Jack's hands and started to put cuffs on him.

"You didn't finish patting me down," Jack pointed out. "You should do that. Not that I'd do anything, but your boss is watching."

"Shut up," Kenny snapped.

"I'm just trying to help," Jack slurred. "Because, if I was a bad guy, I could just swing around, grab your gun and…BANG." Jack's arms went out.

"Close your mouth." Kenny struggled to cuff Jack with Jack gesturing drunkenly.

"Sorry, I'm drunk. Have you done this before, Kenny? 'Cause you're doing it all wrong. Let me explain. You…what you do is push me up against the car a little. Not like smash my face, but you push the guy into the car, and it knocks the wind out of them and shuts them up."

Kenny pushed Jack into the car.

Jack laughed. "I said lightly but not like a daisy."

Kenny gave him a hard shove into the cruiser, which knocked the wind out of Jack.

"Good." Jack coughed. "That was much better."

Lights and sirens blared as another cruiser rushed to the scene. It was a white Crown Victoria with a bubble light attached to the roof. Following right behind it was an ambulance.

"Damn. That's gotta be the chief," Jack said.

Kenny nodded.

A middle-aged cop in a white shirt approached, and Jack tried to keep his eyes focused.

"You got everything under control?" the chief called to Kenny as he marched over to Nelson.

"Yes, sir." Kenny nodded.

"I have the scene contained, Dennis," Nelson said to the chief.

Dennis pointed at Terry sitting on the ground. "Sure looks it."

Nelson brought the chief up to speed on the situation.

The ambulance doors shut with a loud clang. Two EMTs walked over. Each carried a large bag. The younger one walked over to Terry. The older one walked over to Jack.

"Evening, Kenny." The man set the emergency bag down. He was in his early fifties with salt-and-pepper hair and a handlebar mustache. He was five foot ten and trim.

"Hey, Dale." Kenny waved.

Dale put rubber gloves on as he looked at Jack. "Where are you hurt?"

"I'm just tired." Jack grinned lopsidedly.

"You're obviously drunk." Dale frowned. "But you're cut as well."

Jack stumbled as he tried to look himself over for any cuts. "No, I'm not."

Dale pointed at Jack's shirt. "You're bleeding."

"It's not my blood." Jack jerked his head in Terry's direction. "It's his."

"Do you require medical assistance?" Dale asked, now obviously annoyed.

"Yeah." Jack nodded. "Do you have something so I can sleep? Some kinda pill?"

"Who?" the chief yelled at Terry.

Jack looked over.

Terry was gesturing wildly but Jack couldn't hear what he was saying. Terry pointed and everyone turned to stare at Jack.

"Oh, crap." Jack groaned. "That's no good."

The chief stormed over to Jack, followed closely by Nelson. The chief was about five eight with a large potbelly. Sandy-brown hair poked out from under his blue cap. As he searched Jack's face, his eyes went wide. "I'll be damned," he muttered.

"What?" Jack shrugged.

The chief grabbed Jack's wallet from Kenny. He flipped it open to reveal the license and badge. "Jack Stratton? You're on the job? Darrington?"

"I was on the job. After this gets back to my boss, I'm not so sure."

"Is it true? You look just like him. Patty's your mother?" the chief asked.

Jack made a move that resembled a nod but because it caused everything to spin, he tried to just hold his head still.

"When Terry told me, I thought either he was crazy or you were but...wait here." The chief and Nelson walked back to Terry.

Dale grabbed his bag. "I'll note that he's drunk and uninjured," he huffed to Kenny before he walked over to his partner.

"Does that mean I don't get a pill?" Jack called after him.

Dale glared back over his shoulder.

The chief, Nelson, and Terry exchanged words. Terry's face was swollen and bloody. Jack was surprised he was able to stand.

After a few moments, the chief and Nelson walked back while the EMTs looked after Terry.

Halfway, Nelson stepped in front of Dennis. "It's assault. You can't just let him walk."

"He needs a couple of Band-Aids. He gets worse at hockey. Besides, it's my call, Frank. You heard Terry. He's not pushing for charges."

"That's irrelevant. We know that an assault occurred—"

"No, we don't and if Terry doesn't want to say one did, it's over. Did you hear Terry say that he deserved a crack in the mouth?"

"Just because this guy says he's Steven's son doesn't mean that we just let him walk."

"No. If he is Steven's son, it does mean that." The chief pulled up his belt and his stomach jiggled. "You and me both owe him at least that."

Dennis started forward but Nelson stepped in front of him again. Nelson lowered his voice. "Stick him in the drunk tank for tonight then. In the morning, we can make sure that he leaves town. That's the call I would make."

"You're not the chief anymore. I am. So it's my call." Dennis pulled his hat lower and walked around Nelson.

"Uncuff him," Dennis ordered as he walked up to Kenny.

Kenny looked over to Nelson, and Dennis's nostrils flared.

"Uncuff him, now, Kenny." Dennis pointed at Jack.

"Yes, sir." Kenny uncuffed Jack.

"Make sure Terry gets home okay," Dennis instructed. As Kenny walked away, Dennis turned to Jack. "Dennis Wilson. I was a friend of your dad's."

Jack shook his hand but wobbled. "Jack Stratton."

"What the hell are you doing, son?" Dennis put his arm around Jack's shoulder and led him over to the passenger side of the cruiser.

"I'm drunk."

"And stupid. Frank wanted me to take you in. He said that he already pulled you over—"

"That's crap. She stopped. What's his problem?"

"Frank's got a chip on his shoulder but don't worry about him. He works for me. Why'd you pick a fight with Terry?"

"Because I'm trying to fall asleep," Jack muttered as he got in.

"Stay with me, Jack. Now, I got Terry not to press charges, but…" Dennis walked over to the driver's side. He pulled the bubble light off the roof and stuck it back on the dashboard.

Jack tapped the light. "I have to get one for my car."

"Good luck. They don't make them anymore. That was my dad's." He grinned. "Just like Starsky and Hutch."

Jack pressed the button, and lights flashed and the loud siren filled the inside of the car. The chief fumbled with the switch and it shut off.

"Sit your butt back. You've caused enough problems tonight."

"Everything alright?" Nelson called over as he stood next to Kenny and Terry beside the other police cruiser.

"It's fine, Frank," Dennis yelled back. "Kenny, get Terry home now." Dennis started the car and pulled out of the lot.

"Frank's got an attitude." Jack fumbled with his seat belt.

"He's a good cop and he's been on the force longer than you've been alive. Show some respect."

"Sorry," Jack mumbled.

"Where are you staying?"

"Hope Falls Inn."

"That's close."

"Maybe I should go someplace else." Jack nodded. "She's going to be all mad."

"Who's going to be mad?"

"I tried to find out about her, but now she's pissed." Jack tossed his hands up.

"Her who?"

"Replacement. She's all…" Jack scrunched up his face and held up his hands like claws. "Roar. Angry. She cried. I hate that…"

"What the hell are you talking about, son?"

"Alice. I ran a background check…" Jack's hands went up and out. "Now she's totally nuts."

"You ran a background check on the girl you're here with? And you don't get why she's ticked off? Maybe you did fall a little far from the tree."

"She didn't want me to come here…but I'm gonna do this."

"You must be a charmer. Why are you in Hope Falls?"

"I'm looking."

"Looking?"

"For the guy who killed my father."

Dennis sighed. His shoulders drooped, along with his voice. "Jack, we never found the guy. Is that why you went after Terry?"

"No. He said something about…" Jack shrugged. "I felt like hitting him."

Dennis frowned. "Everyone wants to hit Terry sometimes, but being a cop, you should know better than that."

"I don't know jack." Jack's head thumped against the window, and he laughed. "Get it? I don't know me."

"You're not going to find yourself at the bottom of a bottle." Dennis turned right.

"I'm going to find the guy who killed Steven. It's up to me. Cops have nothing. Cops did nothing."

Dennis slammed the brakes on the car, and Jack caught himself on the dashboard.

"My father worked that case. He worked it like it was his own son who got killed, so don't you dare say that he didn't do all he could."

Jack leaned back against the window and turned his head to look at Dennis. "Your father? That's right. He was chief then. Sorry. All I know is what I read in the stupid paper."

"Well, you need the facts and not what you read in the papers." He shook his head. "The paper here? Birds don't even want to crap on it."

"Facts? How do I get the facts? You said... Hey! You can get me stuff. Facts." Jack tapped Dennis's chest.

"If you want to know, I'll bring you up to speed. We never closed the case."

"Let's go." Jack pointed straight ahead but then looked around, confused. "Where's the police station?"

"I'm not going to talk with you about it when you're three sheets to the wind." Dennis turned in to the inn parking lot.

Jack held onto the dashboard. "Well, I got nothing, so I need help. Nothing. Nadda. Zilchie."

Dennis put the cruiser in park and frowned at Jack. "Sleep it off. I'll stop by tomorrow."

Jack got out of the cruiser and held onto the door. "Thank you," he slurred, before he stumbled up the steps.

The lobby was empty, and he had to hold onto the railing as the room moved. Even with one eye open, he couldn't get things to straighten out. The room door squeaked as he staggered through. Replacement rushed up to him but she quickly made a face as though she smelled a skunk. She stepped back. "Have you been drinking?"

"Drinking? No. I drank. I drink...drunk."

"Jack, I...can you stand right here?" She tapped her foot on the floor next to the bed. Jack walked in a curvy line to the spot and stopped.

He heard her close the door.

"Look at me."

Jack's eyes went wide as he tried to pivot around, and his upper body swung in a wide arc. He grinned lopsidedly as he straightened up to face her; the backs of his legs almost touched the bed. Replacement slammed both hands into his chest, which knocked him onto the bed. Jack groaned from the impact and landed with his arms outstretched. He struggled to sit up, but she grabbed his foot first and peeled his shoe off.

"Shut up," she snapped as she yanked the other shoe off, too.

"I'm an idiot."

"Yes, you are." She walked around to the top of the bed. "Sit up."

Jack struggled to slide back while Replacement grabbed him and peeled his shirt off. She made a face as she tossed it in the corner.

Her hands on his belt made him gasp. "Hold—"

She smacked his hand away. "I said, shut up." She yanked his belt open and undid the button on his pants. "Roll over." Replacement groaned as she pulled him onto his stomach.

"Sorry," he mumbled into the soft sheets that warmed his face.

"I have a feeling you will be." She peeled his jeans off.

Jack tried to say something else, but the bed was so soft and he was so tired that sleep finally found him.

CHAPTER 20

How Did I Get Out Of My Clothes?

Jack opened one eye and groaned. His head hurt so badly he didn't want to move. He tried to remember the details from the night before.

Stupid background check. The bar. Lots of drinks. Terry Bradford. Damn. Cops. Nelson. I'm so screwed.

Jack sat up and rubbed his face. His mouth tasted like mothballs.

I need a shower.

Jack groaned as he rolled off the bed, swaying unsteadily when he stood. His stomach turned. He looked down at his pants on the floor and frowned.

How did I get out of my clothes?

After Dennis dropped him off, everything was a complete blank. He held onto the furniture as he stumbled to the bathroom. Surrounded by blankets and pillows, Replacement sat up in the tub and rubbed her eyes.

"You're awake. I hoped you'd sleep longer," she said groggily.

"Did you sleep in the tub?"

"Not too well." She frowned.

"I'm sorry. I was an ass." Jack held out his hand. "Let me help you."

"Look at your hand."

"Ah…" Jack looked down at his swollen hand, noting the dried blood he was sure didn't belong to him.

"You didn't." She glared at him.

"I didn't start it."

"Who?"

"Terry Bradford. He came into the bar and got in my face."

"How is he?"

"Breathing."

Her eyes widened. "Hospital?"

Jack shook his head. "The cops came."

"Cops? Did you get arrested?"

"No."

"You didn't do anything to the cops?"

Jack winced at her raised voice. "No. It was Dennis Wilson, the chief. The guy Terry Martinez told us about."

"Did you ask him anything?"

"I don't know." Jack rubbed his face.

"What? Did he ask you anything?"

"I screwed up." He leaned against the sink. "I can't remember. I'm an idiot."

"Yeah. You said that, and I still agree. Go soak your head." She carried the bedding out.

Jack took his time in the shower. He waited until the last of the hot water ran out. He didn't want to get out. Eventually the cold water won, and Jack retreated from his sanctuary. As the water stopped, he heard voices in the room. He quickly put on his pants and opened the bathroom door. Chief Wilson sat in the chair, and Replacement was on the edge of the bed.

Dennis stood and stared at Jack. "Damn, boy. You look just like your old man." He stuck out his hand. "I was talking to your girl here, and she told me you ain't been sleeping. You've been having nightmares and such, so you decided to go looking for your father."

Jack resisted the urge to look at Replacement and nodded. "Sorry about last night."

"You got nothing to be sorry for. I heard what he said about Patty. Sounds like he deserved a punch in the jaw."

Jack nodded.

"I was Steve's friend, Jack. If you need help, just ask. He'd have done anything for me. What can I do for you?"

Replacement cleared her throat.

Jack held up a hand. "I've been flying blind. Do you know the case?"

"I'm the chief. Of course I know the case. You got something new?"

Jack gave a brief shake of his head. This time he looked at Replacement, who gave a small understanding nod.

"No. It's like Alice said. I've just been thinking about it. I decided to come and check into it."

The chief sighed. "Well, I'm glad to help then. I don't know if you remember last night, but you said you had nothing to go on except what you read in the papers. I had my secretary copy the case files. They're on the bureau."

Jack looked at the pile of manila folders. It was eight inches high.

"Thank you."

"Before I give them to you, I need you to be straight with me, and I'll be straight with you. You're a cop and Steve's son, so I'm giving you some leeway, but before you do anything, you talk to me. If you go off again, there'll be consequences."

"I get it."

"Do you? I know your boss, Sheriff Collins. That guy is so by the book, I think he has it shoved—" He looked at Replacement and cleared his throat. "From what you've said, this is a lot for anyone to handle all at once. Are you sure you're okay with it?" He glanced at the police reports.

"I got it." Jack rubbed the sides of his head.

"Maybe we should just take it easy. Treat this like a real vacation," Replacement said.

Jack leaned against the doorway. "What am *I* supposed to do on vacation?"

"You fish?" Dennis asked.

"Fish? Well…not since high school."

"Go get a fishing rod and take a break. We've got some of the best fishing around."

Jack saw Replacement's worried face. He nodded. "Where?"

"You drove over Mill Brook River when you got off the highway. Head back that way and take a right before the bridge. There's a little pond. Your dad and I used to go there all the time. There's a path that goes all the way around. On the right, there are two large rocks and right there is the deep spot. Catfish big as your arm."

"Got it."

"A little before the bridge is Ron's Bait, Tackle, and Sports. You can get some gear there. After you go fishing, if you still want to, we'll talk."

"Okay."

Dennis waved to Replacement. "Nice to meet you."

"Nice to meet you too."

Jack walked Dennis to the door and held out his hand. "Thank you, again. I appreciate you smoothing things over with Terry."

Dennis shook his hand. "Keep an eye on him, sweetie." He winked at Replacement and walked out.

Replacement went to the folders. "Do you want something to eat before we go fishing?"

"I'm good." Jack moved over to the desk and switched on the lamp.

"I'll be right back."

Jack hesitated for a moment. He wanted to find his father's killer, but he didn't want to know what was in those files.

He took a deep breath and opened it up. The first paper was a crime-scene photo. Steven lay on his back—his eyes were closed, bruises covered his face, his shirt and his pants were soaked in blood. Jack's stomach churned; he snapped the file closed.

God... Please help me.

He closed his eyes and started to shake. He'd looked at a thousand different crime-scene photos; all of them left their mark, but these weren't of some stranger—they were of his father.

Jack tried to pull himself together. A few minutes later, Replacement came in with a tray of food.

"We'll eat something, and then—Jack?" Replacement saw his grim expression. She rushed over and knelt beside his chair. "Oh, Jack…"

Jack sat up and ran his fingers through his hair. "I've seen three different pictures of my father. Only three." He flipped open the folder. "Look at the third."

Replacement looked but then quickly closed it. "Jack, I'm so sorry." She touched the back of his head. She lifted the folders and moved the pile over to the bed behind him.

"I need to get through this. I should see the photos."

"You can see the photos tomorrow." She rubbed his shoulder as she put down a folder. Jack reached for it, but before he could open it, Replacement stopped his hand.

"At least let me see the police reports."

"Only if you promise to take a break this afternoon and do something else."

Jack nodded.

Reluctantly, she picked up the folder and leafed through it before she handed him the report.

The official police report was photocopied, but it still looked old. Jack read the details and Replacement wrote them in the notebook.

I can do this.

His head pounded, but he forced himself to sit up and keep going.

Three hours later, they had almost as little information as they'd had before. Jack paced the floor. "They came up with no suspects. No enemies. No motives. Nothing. And nothing similar before or since." He stopped pacing.

"I'm sorry, Jack."

"Don't be. We've ruled out a lot with the report." He cracked his neck. "They couldn't figure it out, but we will."

CHAPTER 21

Can they Get Out?

Jack and Replacement walked through the front door of Ron's Bait, Tackle, and Sports. The store was one large room. Jack headed straight for the fishing section.

"This place is huge." Replacement picked up a big, floppy hat with mosquito netting. "The bugs must have teeth out here."

Jack chuckled. "There won't be any out now." He picked up a fishing kit made to go in the back of the car trunk. It came with a collapsible rod and all the tackle that he'd need. "Do you want your own rod?"

Replacement made a face as if he offered her a flu shot. "No thanks. That's real cute." She pointed to a female mannequin in a pink wet suit. "Where would you use that around here?"

"Big Bear Run," a short man said with a large smile as he limped past them. "It's just ten miles down the interstate. Largest lake in the state. Welcome to Ron's. I'm Ron."

"A little too cold for me." Jack followed Ron to the back counter. "I'll just take this and a dozen worms."

Replacement's face scrunched up.

"Do you want a setup for your girlfriend?" Ron asked. "I got a great starter kit. The rod's purple sparkled."

"Thanks but I don't fish." Replacement shook her head.

Ron reached behind the counter and placed a Styrofoam cup on the counter.

Jack paid for everything and then headed for the car. He put the tackle box and rod in the back and handed the Styrofoam cup to Replacement. "Do you mind holding them?"

"Them?" Her eyebrow ticked up.

"The worms."

She whacked his shoulder with one hand and held the container away from herself. "Gross. Take it back! Take it back!"

Jack took the container back. "I just didn't want it to tip over. Can you put it between your feet?"

She scooted over against the door. "What? Can they get out? No."

Jack started to set them on the seat next to him.

"Not there!" Replacement waved her hands as she shifted as far away as she could. "Put them in the trunk."

"Come on. Don't be so dramatic."

"They're *worms*."

Shaking his head, Jack went and put them in the trunk.

Ten minutes later, the Impala made its way down a narrow road with thick pine trees along both sides. After a few twists and turns, they stopped in a gravel parking lot. Across a grassy field dotted with picnic tables, a little pond sat in the distance. Jack grabbed the fishing rod and worms from the trunk.

As he slammed the trunk shut, he heard the crunch of gravel as a car stopped back down the road. He looked toward the sound, but couldn't see through the trees. Tires churned the gravel as the car turned around and sped off.

"Are you feeling better?" Replacement stretched her arms above her head as she got out of the car.

Jack stared up the road and listened as the unseen car drove away.

"Hello?" She waved her hand, trying to break his trance.

"Sorry." Jack shook his head. "Shower, food, and the aspirin helped. Thank you for not giving me a guilt trip this morning."

Replacement's shoulders scrunched up and her head tipped to the side. "I might talk a lot but I'm not a nagging shrew."

"Any other girl would have smothered me in my sleep last night."

She smirked. "That thought does have some appeal, but you apologized. All's forgiven, east from west."

They walked toward the pond. It was a medium-sized pond with a little wooden dock. Jack headed straight for a wide flat rock that stretched out into the water.

Replacement took Jack's outstretched hand as he helped her onto the rocks. It only took him a few minutes to set up the rod and bait the hook. The line swished as he cast it out toward the center of the pond.

Jack fished in silence while Replacement squatted down and looked out over the water.

"I need to go there," Jack said.

"Where?"

"Buckmaster. I need to see the crime scene."

Replacement sighed. "I thought today you'd take it easy. Just fish."

Jack held his hand out to the still water. "I know but…they didn't dive the pond."

"They dredged it."

"It's not the same. And they didn't do it until spring."

"I'll confirm it when I get to a computer but the police report said that the pond iced over."

Jack nodded. "Still, they should have gone diving. Just dredging it isn't the same."

"Wouldn't it be like looking for a needle in a haystack?" Replacement's shoulders popped up and down.

"Not now. You need to search in a grid. Slowly. They have metal detectors now that are much better, too."

Replacement peered into the water. "Look how clear the water is."

Jack looked over the edge, too. The water was so clear he could see the sandy bottom.

"How deep is it?"

"Right there is only about eight feet." Jack pointed. "Over where I cast I think is deeper. Hold on." He started to reel in his line.

"What are you doing?" Replacement asked.

"I want to get rid of the bobber and bottom fish. It's deep. Look how still the water is. It's perfect for catfish."

Replacement folded her hands in front of herself and smiled.

"Do you want a turn?" Jack held out the rod.

Replacement hesitated but he noticed the slightest curl of her lip. "No thanks. You fish."

"You're going to be bored just watching me. Do you want to walk around?"

"Do you mind?"

"I'm fishing." Jack smiled. "You can do whatever you want."

"Thanks." She hopped off the rock. "I'll follow this trail." She pointed to a path that ran straight up a little hill.

Jack cast out the line again and watched it disappear. He kept his finger loose on the line, feeling it as it continued to slide out. Finally, the line stopped.

He looked back to see Replacement standing at the top of the hill. She waved and then continued out of sight. Jack brushed back his hair and made a face. His head still pounded.

Jack's rod twitched in his hands. He gave a firm, quick tug to set the hook, and the rod bent over. He smiled as he reeled in. It was sluggish. He stopped and looked at the end of the rod. It was now curving toward the water. He waited. The rod didn't move.

Dang. I must have caught a log.

He reeled it in slowly, and the line suddenly went crazy. The gears on the cheap reel slipped and the line started going back out.

The tension is wrong! I forgot to set it.

Jack tried to adjust the tension as he struggled with the fish on the end of the line. He moved forward and looked down. From the depths, he could see a massive catfish trying to escape back into the darkness. A crack in the rod caused him to lower the tip and reel faster.

"Yes," he cheered as he dragged the hulking fish onto the rock. It was an enormous, fat catfish. It flopped on the rock and twisted. Jack quickly grabbed the cold, slimy fish and marveled at its size. He was sure it was the largest fish he'd ever caught. After a bit of twisting, Jack managed to free his prize from the hook. He gently tossed it back into the water. With three powerful flicks of its tail, it disappeared back into the blackness.

Jack shivered as he washed his hands in the water, and then he froze, not because of the cold, but because of his reflection. As the ripples faded and the water calmed, he stared at himself. He realized his father must have done the same thing in the exact same place.

Steven wasn't anything like what I thought he'd be. He wasn't some guy sleeping with a prostitute. He was just a kid. Seventeen. I had him all wrong...

Jack looked back for Replacement, but she was nowhere to be seen. Leaving the rod, he jumped down from the rocks and jogged up the path after her. At the crest of the hill, he came up short. A beautiful field spread out before him. The grass looked like waves frozen in time. In the middle of the field was a large oak tree. Jack saw its branches move. When he saw a foot dangle, he laughed. Replacement had climbed up into its branches.

"Having fun?"

"Jack, this is the best climbing tree ever."

He grabbed a low, thick branch, and hung for a moment. He felt like a kid again. He pulled himself up and sat on the branch next to her.

Jack watched her. Her smile was as open to interpretation as the *Mona Lisa*'s.

"It's a romantic spot." She pointed to the trunk, and Jack noticed the places all over it where the bark had been removed. "You should see some of these. CR loves KD or Billy loves Wendy forever and ever. It's cute."

"Must be a local tradition."

"I found one that may be something."

"May be something?" Jack hoisted himself higher to get a better look.

"DJ + PC." She pointed to a large heart that at one time had three arrows in it, but two of the ends were broken off.

"PC—do you think that's Patty Cole?" Replacement asked.

Jack shook his head. "It could also be Penelope Cruz. You ready?"

"Did you catch anything?" She started down.

"Yeah." Jack smiled smugly. "A giant catfish."

"Where is it?"

"I put it back."

"You put it back in the pond? Then why did you try to catch it?"

"That's the point. I just like trying to catch them. It's the hunt. Race you."

Jack jogged for the hill. Replacement was in shape, but he'd never seen her run. She blazed past him. Jack quickly changed into a sprint. Startled by her speed, he pushed himself to go faster, but she was already going over the crest of the hill. She was small, but her little legs were a blur. Jack made it to the rock first but not by much.

"Crud, I almost beat you!" She bent at the waist and gulped in air. "We need to run more. As a cop, you should be super fast."

"I am fast."

"But you should be super fast." She struck a pose like she was frozen mid-sprint. "Like the Flash. Cops are supposed to be able to run super fast, right?"

Jack grinned. "That's why we have guns and cars."

She laughed. "Where to now?" She skipped a rock across the pond.

"I thought of something. I want to go back over the police report." Jack walked back.

"Are you sure?"

"Yeah."

"And tonight?"

"Let's get something to eat at the inn." Jack smiled.

"That's great. Uh…at the inn? I could…"

"Or we can get delivery. Whatever you want." He grinned. He knew she loved delivery. "Can you hold the rod and tackle box?"

"Sure." Replacement looked perplexed. "If we eat at the inn, I just want to go back and change—"

"Stop for a second." Jack walked backward. "Just hold up right there." A grin slowly spread across his face as he continued to back up. "Race you to the car."

He turned and bolted.

"Cheater," Replacement cursed as she sprinted after him.

Jack didn't look behind him as he flew ahead. He hoped the pole and tackle box would be enough to ensure his win, and he was right. As he reached the woodchip path, he was surprised to hear Replacement so close behind. When the Impala came into view, Jack froze and skidded to a stop.

"You can't let me win now, you—" Replacement slammed to a stop when she saw the car.

The Impala leaned at an odd angle—all four tires had been slashed. Jack protectively moved in front of Replacement. Besides them, the area seemed deserted.

Replacement wasn't scared; she was outraged. "It's a warning. They want to scare us off."

Jack scanned the woods and the corner of his mouth ticked up. "We're getting closer. Someone's getting nervous. They're getting scared."

"What do we do now?"

"We keep digging."

CHAPTER 22
Steak and Cheese, Baby!

The tow truck took over an hour to get to the pond. It was another hour before the new tires were on and they could leave. When they finally returned to the inn, it was getting dark. As they headed up the walkway, Replacement turned to look back at the car and then exhaled. "I thought you'd be beyond crazy mad about your car, but I have to give it to you, you didn't flip out."

Jack kept walking but smiled. "I guess that was sort of a compliment?"

"Yeah. I mean…you love that car. You've been super short-fused, so what gives?"

Jack stopped and looked back at the car for a second. "Someone followed us out to the pond."

"They did?"

"Yeah…I heard a car pull down the road but I just thought it was someone backing up."

"And why would this make you happy?"

"That means I'm rattling someone's cage."

"In general, or in regards to investigating the murder?"

"I'm hoping the latter."

"Do you smell that?" Replacement moaned as the odor of a roast drifted out from the inn.

They walked through the front door and Jack stopped, but Replacement kept walking a few steps. Kristine Jenkins stood at the desk and stared at Jack. She pressed her lips tightly together but the corners briefly twitched up.

"Head up to the room," Jack whispered to Replacement. "Order whatever you want to eat."

"Are you okay?" Replacement asked, not taking her eyes off Kristine.

"I'm fine. Go order something to eat."

Replacement held her ground.

Kristine took a step toward them. "Jack. Can I speak to her for a second?"

Jack's mouth fell open. *Why does she want to talk to Replacement?* "Um…"

Before he could think of a response, Replacement marched forward. Kristine escorted Replacement around the corner. A few moments later, Replacement returned; her eyes were wide.

Jack gawked at her, puzzled.

Replacement swallowed. "I think you should go talk to her."

"I'm not sure I want to." Jack didn't move.

"I…I'd like to explain," Kristine said. "There's something I need to talk with you about."

If this chick goes psycho again…

Jack looked down at Replacement, but she only nodded again. He exhaled and followed Kristine into the same room, but he paused in the doorway. A tray with four teacups and assorted cookies sat on the table.

"Please sit down." Kristine motioned to the couch.

Jack stayed in the doorway. He pointed at the teacups. "Are we expecting company?"

"I didn't know if your friend would be joining us."

"That still leaves a cup."

"It's for a friend of mine." Kristine held up a hand.

Jack noticed her hand shook. He stepped into the room and shut the door.

"I…I want to apologize for my behavior the other night." She slightly bowed her head. "I don't normally behave that way, but there was…something about you." Her eyes searched his but it was the look on her face that made Jack's chest tighten. "When you kissed me, and I looked into your eyes…" She inhaled deeply and her lip quivered. "I couldn't understand how it could be. Your eyes were the same as someone I knew." She rubbed her trembling hands together. "Steven Ritter."

Jack sat down.

"When I first saw you, I thought I was losing my mind. I thought you resembled him, nothing more, and I was being foolish."

Jack swallowed, unsure what to say.

"It was so long ago, but I'll never forget his eyes. When I looked into yours… I knew Steven didn't have any kids, but maybe you were a distant relative. I didn't know what to do. I've always been close with Mrs. Ritter, so—"

Jack leapt to his feet. "The other cup. Is she here?"

Kristine held up her hand. "She is. You're Steven Ritter's son."

"Yes. You knew my father?"

She nodded. "We dated all through high school."

Jack sat back down.

"I was a grade above him. I went to college and…called it off." She wrung her hands. "How?"

Jack shifted uncomfortably. "How?"

"You?"

"Do you mean who?"

"I'm sorry. Yes. Who? Who's your mother?"

Jack hesitated. From the reactions he was getting around town, he didn't want to see that same look on Kristine's face when he said Patty's name.

"Patricia Cole."

"Patty." She closed her eyes.

"Aren't you going to say something about her? Everyone else in this town has."

"Who am I to judge? I know Patty had it rough. It's just that…that's how Steven was. He had a soft spot for the hard-luck cases." Tears rolled down her face.

Jack started to rise and she held up a hand.

"Don't. If I start crying, I won't stop." She quickly rose and marched over to the far door. She paused for a moment, straightened her dress and wiped her eyes. "Are you ready to meet her?"

Jack sat up, and then nervously nodded.

A brief, sympathetic smile crossed her face, and she opened the door. A moment later, Mrs. Ritter slowly walked into the room. Jack moved to the center of the room, and the old woman trembled as she approached. Her blue eyes stared at Jack.

"I'm sorry I didn't tell you in the store—"

In disbelief, she walked forward and gently touched his arm.

"I'm sorry." Jack began again, but the old woman clutched him to her and began to weep.

Kristine quietly left the room.

"What's your name?" Mrs. Ritter asked.

"Jack Stratton."

"Who…who's your mother?"

Slowly, Jack told her his whole life story. Jack decided to include it all, so he told her about being left at the bus station, Aunt Haddie's, and his adopted parents. The summation of his life took over an hour. He could see that the old woman fought to hold back tears.

"Why? I don't understand why she didn't tell me…" Her voice trailed off.

"She was pretty messed up. I don't know why she kept me so long."

She pulled Jack close. "I'd never have let you go."

Jack held the old woman while she cried some more. She sat up and wiped her eyes with a tissue.

As she looked at him, her lip began to tremble once more. "Steven would have been so proud." She let out a large sob. The door suddenly popped open, and Kristine and Replacement tumbled into the room. The two straightened up and tried not to look guilty.

"Well, since you're already in the room." Jack gestured toward Mrs. Ritter.

Replacement cleared her throat and took a step forward. "I'm Alice."

"Nice to meet you, my dear." Mrs. Ritter shook her outstretched hand. "I'm feeling a little overwhelmed."

"We don't have to do this all at once." Jack stood.

Mrs. Ritter grabbed his hand. "Please, I'd just like to talk some more…would you come and visit? I can make you lunch?" The panicked woman struggled for words as she pulled herself up.

"That would be fine." Jack gave her a reassuring smile while Kristine moved over and placed her arm around the old woman's shoulders.

"I know where you live. I'll get your number from Kristine. I'll stop by soon."

"Okay."

Jack relaxed as she hugged him, long and hard.

"When will you come to see me?" Mrs. Ritter squeezed his elbow.

"This week."

Mrs. Ritter smiled, and then Kristine walked her out the door.

Replacement and Jack watched them go while Jack put his hand on the doorframe. "Are you hungry?"

"I'm starving." Replacement spun around.

"You could have grabbed something to eat in the dining room."

"I waited for you. I didn't know what you were doing with 'the dancer.'" She wobbled her head and struck a pose.

"Knock it off. What did you have delivered?"

"I ordered subs. Steak and cheese, baby." Replacement raced up the stairs.

Jack looked out the door, but Kristine's car was long gone.

An hour and a half later, Jack stood up and yawned. Replacement was already pulling the blankets off the bed. A lopsided smile appeared on her face as she picked up a pillow.

"Don't." Jack kicked off his shoes.

"Care to elaborate?"

"You can sleep in the bed." Jack grabbed some sweats and headed for the bathroom.

"And have you toss and turn all night and have another nuclear meltdown? I'll take the tub."

She picked up the pile of bedding, but Jack stopped her in the doorway and held his hand up like a cop directing traffic. "Sleep on your side. We'll put a pillow barrier between us."

"Really?" She lifted herself up on her tiptoes, squeezed the pillow tightly to her chest so her dimples got even bigger.

"Yeah…"

Replacement quickly divided the bed with a rolled-up blanket down the middle. She dashed by him into the bathroom. Jack slipped under the covers. As he lay on his back and stared up at the ceiling, he relaxed. Slowly, he settled into the softness as the warmth of the bed radiated into his body.

I have a grandmother. Weird.

Replacement dashed out of the bathroom and scurried onto her side. She tossed the comforter up and slipped underneath before it fell back down. The whole bed vibrated as she wiggled around until she was comfortable.

"Isn't this bed awesome?" Replacement whispered.

Jack's eyelids were so heavy he could barely lift them. "It is. Can I ask you a question?" Jack opened one eye to find Replacement's face right next to his. He pulled his face back. "I'm glad they have toothbrushes."

"Me too. It's a really good one. I thought, free? It's going to be one of those that fall apart and the bristles get stuck in your teeth. You know what I mean?"

Jack smiled as he struggled to keep his eyes open.

"Was that your question?"

"No. I have two."

"What's your first question?" She leaned closer.

"Is there like a Grandmother's Day?"

"Aww." Replacement set her chin onto her hand, and her lower lip stuck out. "You're so sweet. I'm sure there is. I'll look it up. What's the second?"

"How did you end up at Aunt Haddie's?"

Replacement stared at his face for several minutes and then closed her eyes. "My parents died. That's it. One minute I was in the happiest little family: my mom, dad, and my two little brothers, Andrew and Alex. One minute we were happy, and the next…it was a car accident. I don't remember it. Someone coming the other way fell asleep. They died, too.

"I woke up in the hospital alone. I wasn't even badly hurt. I just wanted to go home. They said I couldn't. My parents' parents were all dead. No brothers or sisters. So, I became a ward of the state. It was so…weird. My parents were really nice. They owned a flower shop. They did everything together. My dad treated me like a princess. He'd bring home a flower for me every day. We didn't have a lot of money. At least that's what I was told. No savings."

She shrugged and rolled back over to look at Jack. "I didn't have it bad like you," she whispered.

"Me? I didn't have it bad. You were eleven. No one tried to…you know…to adopt you?"

"Of course they did. I'm a prize." She struck a funny pose. Her voice changed back to serious. "I was nine when they died. I went…to a different place…before Aunt Haddie's."

"Where was that?" Jack looked up at the ceiling. There was a long pause but he could hear the change in her breathing. It was strained.

"It was a bad place."

Jack didn't need to look at her to know she was fighting back tears.

"I don't like to talk about it. It doesn't matter. They sent me to Aunt Haddie's. She tried to get me adopted. A few times they had a couple come out to look at me. By that time, though, you and Chandler were in the army and, well, Aunt Haddie needed me, and I really loved her. So when potential parents met me, I sorta acted a little weirder than normal so they wouldn't take me…if you know what I mean?"

Jack lay there and listened to his heartbeat.

Life is hard. Hard for a lot of people. Alice has a heart of gold in spite of it. Something happened to her at the first house. Something real bad. She didn't let it define her like I do. What am I doing?

Jack closed his eyes hard and tried to breathe slowly. "You're a good person." His voice was low, and his throat was tight.

"Jack?"

"Yeah?"

"Thanks for asking."

CHAPTER 23

The Widow's Walk

Replacement moaned, which caused Jack to turn around. Her arm was draped over the rolled-up blanket that had served as their nighttime barrier. She pulled it closer, and her leg rose up as she purred again.

Jack cracked his neck and took a deep breath. The sound of her sigh seemed almost too low for her little body; it resonated deep within her chest. Jack smiled, but as he turned back to the desk to work, his eyes caught a glimpse of her thigh. He closed his eyes and turned around, but another soft moan made him rethink.

Don't go there, Jack...

He coughed. Loudly.

Replacement's eyes flew open.

"Good morning."

"I, uh...I...you're up," she stammered. Replacement pulled the comforter around her as the color rose in her cheeks. "Good morning."

"How'd you sleep?"

"Great! Did you like sleeping with me?" She froze mid-stretch. "I meant, I liked sleeping with you. I meant you...I enjoyed it... How'd you sleep?"

Jack grinned as he kept his eyes focused on his work. "I slept great."

Replacement slipped out of bed and hurried for the bathroom.

Jack grabbed another yearbook and opened it on the desk. He started at the beginning of the book again and carefully scanned each page.

What're you missing, Jack?

He had learned long ago to trust that "check" inside him. Call it what you want: intuition, Spidey-sense, or a gut feeling; he trusted it. Every time he even thought about the yearbook, he got that feeling. He studied each face in every photo and read every typed word. His hand stopped on page fifteen.

No way...

Jack glared down at the picture of a man, in his late twenties, dressed in a dark suit and tie. His light-brown hair was on the longer side, and he had a dashing smile. TERRANCE WATKINS, GUIDANCE COUNSELOR.

Replacement came out of the bathroom, drying her hair. "Whatcha find?"

"A guidance counselor named Terry. Patty was a kid in trouble. She may have gone to him."

Replacement leaned over to look at the picture. "A teacher?" Her finger jabbed the yearbook. "He's, like, way older. What a dirtbag."

"Let's not jump to conclusions, but I'll call Cindy."

Replacement stamped her foot. "I can't believe I didn't bring my laptop."

"It's not a big deal."

"Wait a minute. I want to go check something." Replacement went out of the room.

"Hold up." Jack grabbed his keys and hurried after her.

"Do you think Kristine has a computer?" Replacement said as she disappeared down the staircase.

Jack thumped down the stairs after her and called out, "I don't think the original colonists had the Internet, so that would be—"

He stopped when he saw Kristine at the front desk, frowning up at him. She was talking to an older man with salt-and-pepper hair and a handlebar mustache.

Jack clicked his tongue. "That was…just a little historical joke."

Replacement smiled at Kristine and pointed back at Jack. "Was his dad a wise guy too?"

"Sure was." Kristine nodded.

The man with the mustache turned to Kristine. "Can I have a word with you?" He scowled at Jack.

Kristine walked over to the front door with him. The man was obviously agitated. He spoke in a low rumble. Jack couldn't hear what he was saying but from the way he kept pointing at Jack, he assumed that it was about him.

The man's aggressive stance didn't seem to affect Kristine at all. Her lips were pressed together in a suppressed smile while she nodded her head as if she were humoring a toddler having a tantrum.

The man put his hands on his hips and raised an eyebrow, waiting for her response.

Kristine smiled and kissed his cheek.

The man cast another scowl in Jack's direction and left.

Jack's eyebrow rose as he watched the man walk away. "I've seen him before," Jack said to Kristine as she walked up.

"I just heard all about it. He gave me an earful about watching out for you. You met him the other night."

"The EMT." Jack groaned.

"His name's Dale and he's my overprotective big brother. You didn't make the best first impression."

Jack rubbed the back of his neck. "I don't imagine that I did."

"Did you guys need something?" Kristine asked.

"I was wondering." Replacement pressed her hands together. "Do you have a computer?"

"There's one back in the office." Kristine looked playfully at Jack. "Next to the telegraph machine."

Replacement laughed.

Kristine walked behind the front desk, and they followed.

"Did you know a Terrance Watkins?" Jack asked as they passed through the middle room and into a small office in the back.

Kristine shook her head and pointed Replacement to a wooden desk with a computer. "The name isn't familiar."

The room was small, with only a desk, a chair, and a tiny filing cabinet in the corner. A window looked out on the backyard and the woods beyond.

"I thought Jack was kidding about a Pilgrim owning this thing." Replacement's lip curled up as she sat down. "This computer is older than me."

"That isn't a high bar to overcome." Kristine smiled.

"Terry Watkins was a guidance counselor." Jack leaned against the desk between the two women.

"Oh, yes. Mr. Watkins." Kristine's nostrils flared. "He was a creep. I remember him, now."

"What about him upsets you?" Jack reached vainly for his notebook that was typically in his chest pocket. He'd left it upstairs. He looked around, and then grabbed a pen and pad off the desk.

"Mr. Watkins started there my senior year. I'll never forget the way he ogled me. He had me sit in this low chair, and then he sat on the edge of the desk."

"So he could look down your shirt," Replacement snapped as she continued to type, never taking her eyes off the screen.

"Seriously?" Jack asked.

Kristine patted Jack's arm. "A lot of guys are scumbags."

"Jack doesn't get it, since he's one of the good ones," Replacement added.

Kristine smiled at him.

"Is this him?" Replacement pointed at the monitor. Jack and Kristine walked around to look.

"That's him. Now he has a bad toupee," Kristine answered.

"It says here he's married. No kids. He's a real-estate salesman now. Give me a few minutes and I'll find out some more." Replacement frantically typed.

Kristine touched her shoulder. "Take your time. I have no idea what you're doing anyway. Jack, would you like to join me for a cup of tea?"

Jack leaned down. "Go to it, computer geek girl. Do you want a cup?"

"Tea? No thanks." Replacement didn't even look up.

"This way." Kristine walked back into the middle room and over to the little table as Jack followed. "I was hoping we could talk."

It's never a good thing when a female says that.

"Okay…" Jack noticed the tremor in her hand as she poured two cups of tea.

Jack moved over to the couch but, before he sat down, Kristine spoke. "Not here, upstairs. I wanted to show you something." Kristine handed him a cup, and her nose wrinkled as she smiled.

"You certainly have piqued my interest." Jack smirked as he followed her.

When they reached the second floor, they crossed a landing to a small, wooden staircase that went up.

"I thought there were only two stories?" Jack peered up.

Kristine grinned. "This way."

When they reached the top of the stairs, Jack exhaled when he saw it.

Kristine grinned broadly, crossed her arms, and gave herself a little squeeze.

"Wow…"

Jack stood in awe as he looked around the room. The widow's walk, that looked at least a hundred years old, was adorned with glass and wrought iron. The iron was fashioned to look like vines and flowers, and it encircled a glass atrium with a breathtaking view of Hope Falls. Jack looked out over the forest, which stretched off into the distance behind the inn.

"This is beautiful."

"It was the reason I bought the inn. I've had to have a lot of work done, but almost none up here." She hugged herself tighter. "It's my favorite place on earth."

"I can see why." Jack turned to look off in all directions. A long field sloped off to the north. Rising hills sparkled in the south and, as he looked west, he could see Buckmaster Pond in the distance.

"Thanks for sharing this with me."

"It wasn't the only reason I wanted to get you alone. I wanted to talk to you about Steven." Kristine placed a hand on his elbow.

"I might need coffee if we're going down that road." Jack swirled the tea in the dainty cup.

"I think you need to know." She walked over to face the forest before she continued. "I take it from what you've said that Patty didn't talk about him and…I know it sounds strange but…I don't want that part of him to not be passed along."

Tears are coming.

Jack took a step forward. She held out a hand.

"You'll hear things about Steven from his mother, and that's a part of him. She'll talk about Steven, the son. Terry Martinez or Dennis can talk about Steven, the friend, but…there's no one else to talk about Steven, the man."

She kept her eyes closed.

"Forgive me if I go on, but please let me. Steven went to my school but I didn't really know him. He was a class under me, and I thought anyone younger than me was…less. What a snob I was. I'd been seeing Bryan Ross. He was a real jerk, but at the time I didn't think I could do any better.

"One Friday night, I was on a date at a little fast-food place downtown. I brought the food back to our table and I dropped Bryan's drink. It spilled all over the table and him. I was trying to clean up the mess, and doing my best not to cry at the same time, when Steven ran over. He started helping me clean up the floor.

"The drink had gone all over Bryan's pants. He called me a stupid bitch. Steven punched him in the mouth." She shook her head. "Bryan ran out to his car and took off. I ran after him, but he was gone. I stood there, crying in the parking lot, until Steven came up and offered to give me a ride home." She closed her eyes and smiled. "I said yes.

"He ran around the corner and came back with his bike." She laughed. "Jack, you and he have the same smirk. He said 'I didn't mean that I'd drive you home, just that I'd give you a ride. Your chariot, my lady,' and he gave a little bow.

"He jogged beside me all the way to my house. We talked while I rode. I never told him I took the long way because I didn't want it to end. I fell in love with him that day."

She opened her eyes, and the corner of her mouth curled into a smile.

"Steven sealed the deal when we got to my street. Bryan had come back looking for me and he saw us. He was too scared of Steven to stop, but he drove by and teased him about not having a car. Steven didn't seem to care. I asked him why. He looked at me and said, 'My dad used to say never be embarrassed if you do your best. My bike is the best I can offer you. Besides, Bryan was too stupid not to treat you like gold. Why would I care what he thinks?'"

Jack put his hand behind his neck and looked at Kristine in the reflection of the glass. The corner of Jack's mouth ticked up. "That kinda sounds like how I'd handle it."

Her smile was a mix of joy and sadness. She nodded.

Kristine continued to talk for over an hour. She shared her personal memories of a man Jack didn't know, but the similarities in their personalities floored him. Many times he found himself fighting back his emotions but, much more often, he smiled. She talked about times when they were alone and the private things they said, but it didn't feel wrong. Jack knew it was her way of passing on Steven's memory. A week ago, Jack had no idea who his birth father was; now he found himself gathering the stories that fell from Kristine's lips and holding them dear.

"And then I went to college..." She opened her eyes and lowered her head.

"You broke up with him before you went?"

She shook her head. "No. We were going to have a long-distance relationship. Steven was confident. He was trusting. But he was wrong."

The silence in the room grew, and she continued to stare out into the forest.

"I called him. I couldn't do it to his face." She shifted her feet. "There wasn't anyone else, but I thought...I thought I was so smart and so special." Tears rolled down her cheeks, and her lip trembled. "My new friends at college said that I could do better, so I broke up with him, but never said why."

"You never told him why?" The words escaped Jack's lips before he could stop them. He could see the impact immediately. She hunched her shoulders, squeezed her arms tightly around herself.

"He came to see me. He drove twelve hours straight to ask me, and I still didn't tell him. What could I say? That I was selfish? That I was a spoiled brat?" She walked forward and leaned against the iron railing.

"He came back two weeks after that. He said he just wanted to know why. I could tell how hurt he was but I just walked away. I walked away from the nicest man I have ever known…to a group of girls whose names I can't even remember. Back then they were so important to me." She leaned her head against the glass. "They were laughing and I joined them. That was the last time I ever saw him."

Jack rubbed at his chest.

"I thought I was so special." She looked up at him. "Do you know why? I thought I was so special because that's how he treated me. That's what he always told me. It was him—he made me feel special."

Jack nodded.

"You don't know how much I regretted it. If I hadn't done that, he never would have…"

She started to cry.

He walked forward. "You told me a lot about my father. I feel like he and I are a lot alike."

She nodded.

"Will you do me a favor?" She looked at him, puzzled. "Close your eyes."

Jack grabbed her by her arms and pulled her tightly against him. She exhaled but kept her eyes closed. He lowered his face until he could feel her breath on his mouth. "Don't think, okay? Thank you for telling me about him. When I spoke to my grandmother, she told me about the breakup. She also told me what Steven said to her." Jack held onto her as he felt a tremble race through her. "Open your eyes."

Kristine opened her eyes and gasped. Tears once again formed, but Jack held her by her arms and pulled her tighter. He stared into her eyes.

"Tell me you're sorry."

Her lip trembled. "I'm so sorry, Steven. Please forgive me."

"All's forgiven," he whispered and smiled. "Close your eyes."

As she did, she let her arms slip around his waist and hold him. Jack cradled her and watched the pattern of the clouds sweep across the floor. He comforted her until he felt her start to straighten. He kissed her forehead. Then he quietly slipped away.

CHAPTER 24

CHAT

When Jack walked into the room, Replacement didn't even look up.

"You're back already?" she asked.

Already? I've been upstairs for two hours.

"You find anything out on Terry Watkins?" he asked.

"Super scumbag. He left guidance counseling after five years. Went into real estate. He's been sued four or five times. Married. No kids, which is a great thing because he's on a whole bunch of dating sites."

"You seriously got all that this morning?"

Jack walked around to look at the monitor. Her fingers were a blur as she continued to type.

"I have a ton and would have even more if it wasn't for this prehistoric paperweight." She thrust both hands at the PC and made a face.

"Where does he live?"

"Smithfield. It's—"

"Two towns over." Kristine smiled as she walked into the room.

Jack nodded his head slightly and searched her eyes.

She mouthed, "*Thank you,*" as she leaned against the desk.

Jack put his hand on Replacement's shoulder. "So, Miss Super-Computer-Genius, any luck?"

The computer beeped, and a window popped up.

HELLO appeared on the screen.

"Oh, snap." Replacement groaned.

"What?" Jack leaned forward.

"He's online."

"Who?"

"Terry Watkins." Replacement tilted her head.

"How do you know that? Is he typing to you?" Jack's voice was clipped.

"He sent me a chat. I didn't think he'd respond so soon."

"Respond? Did you contact him?" Jack asked.

"We need to ask him questions, right?" Replacement's head wobbled back and forth.

"Why don't you ever ask me first?"

"You weren't here." Replacement's hands went out.

"Jack, it's okay." Kristine walked over to the other side of Replacement.

"Okay? The last time she sent someone an email, I got hit by a car."

Kristine let out a little laugh before she realized that he wasn't kidding.

"Well, we did want to contact him." Kristine pointed at the screen, and her mouth flopped open. "Why is my picture in the chat window?"

"I had to make a profile," Replacement answered.

"And you used my picture?"

"It was the only one I had on this computer."

HELLO? PATTY? popped up in the window.

"What do I say to him?" Replacement looked to Jack.

"Patty? Did you say you're Patty Cole?" Jack's hand cut the air and shook as he pointed at the monitor.

"Who else was I going to say I am?" She scrunched up her face.

"You used my picture and pretended to be Patty?" Kristine tapped the monitor.

"Type HELLO," Jack instructed.

Replacement typed HI.

Kristine scowled. "You should have asked me first."

"Kristine, it's okay." Jack smiled, but Kristine glared.

IT'S BEEN A LONG TIME. HOW YOU BEEN?

"Can I say wonderful?" Replacement asked.

"No. She's in an institution." Jack held up a hand. "Why would you say wonderful?"

"He doesn't know that," Replacement countered.

"Type okay. Keep him guessing. Guys like mystery." Kristine leaned forward.

OKAY.

"No, we don't." Jack shook his head.

YOU LOOK GREAT. I'M HEADING TO WORK. R U IN THE AREA?

"What do I say?" Replacement's fingers hovered over the keyboard.

"Say yes." Kristine pointed.

"Say no." Jack leaned in. "If you say yes, he may—"

Replacement typed YES.

Jack's hands shot up. "What the hell? I said type NO."

"It was two votes to one." Replacement stayed focused.

"This isn't a democracy." Jack ran his fingers through his hair.

"It's my computer, so it's a matriarchy." Kristine grinned.

GREAT. I'LL CHAT WITH YOU TONIGHT.

The computer beeped, and the window flashed.

"He's gone."

"Why did you do that?" Jack thrust both hands in the air.

Replacement looked at him, incredulous. She was completely unaware of the can of worms she just opened. "Obviously, I'm trying to help. We want to talk to him, so we go undercover, right?"

"Do you know how much planning goes into an undercover operation? We should have gone over what to say, when, how…"

"Sorry." Replacement pushed back her chair.

"Well, now we've found him." Kristine patted Replacement's back. "Should I leave the computer on?"

Replacement frowned. "I hope the thing lasts the day and doesn't melt through the floor."

"Thanks." Kristine rolled her eyes.

"We need to go." Jack looked at Kristine. "We'll be back later. Can you let me know if he reaches out?"

Kristine nodded and they headed out the door.

CHAPTER 25
Patty's Special Day

Jack had double backed twice to check to see whether anyone was following them again. It was almost eleven when the Impala stopped in front of the rundown ranch house. At one time, the house must have been brown, but the peeling paint hung like scabs all over it. Of the four windows in the front, one still had shutters.

Jack parked along the street instead of the driveway filled with four cars, none of which appeared to have moved in years.

"Are you okay with this?" Replacement cast a worried look Jack's way.

"I'm fine. You've heard what people have said about him. I don't have high expectations," Jack said.

"You shouldn't."

"What're you not telling me?" Jack asked.

"I just... I was talking to Kristine about Patty and there was a rumor around town." She looked up at the ceiling and took a deep breath. "It was more than a rumor. Kristine knows this woman who works at the police station. When Patty was thirteen... It was sexual abuse. Patty's mother reported it. She said it was Patty's father."

Jack's stomach dropped. "Did anything come from it?"

"Patty's mother died. There was an investigation, but Patty was eventually returned to her father."

Jack's eyes looked for something to hit or smash. He ground his teeth together as he clenched and unclenched his hands.

"Jack?"

He shoved the door open and Replacement hurried out. There was no discernible path to the front door, so Jack marched across the yard. The door was in the same shape as the house: peeling paint fell in strips, and only three of the four little panes had glass. One had just a piece of cardboard stuck in it. Jack rapped on the door, and paint chips fluttered to his feet. Instinctively, his arm reached out and he moved Replacement slightly behind him.

No one answered.

More knocking. More paint. The door finally opened a crack.

"What?" A tall, old man glared and blinked through the partly open door. Thick gray hair sat atop a heavily wrinkled face. He shielded his yellow eyes with his hand and stared out suspiciously.

"Mr. Cole? I have a few—"

Jack caught the slamming door and held it in place.

"You're a cop. Get lost," he snarled. His lips drew back to reveal browned teeth.

"I'm not here officially." Jack fumed. "Ten minutes of questions." He pulled out a fifty-dollar bill. "You get another fifty when we're done."

The old man licked his lips as if he were looking at a steak. He grabbed the bill; the door shut, a chain rattled, and then the door flew wide open.

Mr. Cole was Jack's height. He was slightly stooped over, but his old clothes hung around him like a scarecrow. As the musty smell seeped across the threshold, Replacement coughed and made a face. The old man leered at her and grinned. "Why hello, sweetie."

"Don't talk to her."

"You think you can talk to me like that, you—"

"Part of the payment," Jack growled and walked forward, backing the old man up.

The man turned and shuffled into what once was a living room. It was sunny outside, but even though the light was on, it was still dark in the room. Old, thick curtains hung across the windows. There was a small TV in the corner with a worn chair in front of it. A couch with a pile of clothes and assorted trash was against the far wall. The old man shoved the pile over, which created one seat. He headed for the chair.

"What the hell do you want?" he grumbled as he sat down.

"I'm here to ask some questions about Patricia."

"Patricia?"

"Your daughter." Jack seethed. He could see it in the old man's face. No recognition.

"Patty?" He spat out the word. "That bitch took off years ago. Haven't seen her. Don't care."

Replacement started to step forward, but Jack grabbed her arm.

"She's a feisty one." The lecherous grin appeared again. "Is Patty dead? Did she leave me something?" He started to sit up.

"Sit your ass down and look only at me."

The old man's face contorted in anger. His mouth opened but he closed it when Jack took two steps forward.

"Did Patty ever talk about a Steven?"

"A Steven? How the hell am I supposed to know that? What do kids have girlfriends for? To gossip. Why would she tell me crap?"

"Did she ever bring anyone"—Jack looked around the decrepit house with disgust—"here?"

"She wasn't allowed to have anyone over. Ever. It would just cause problems."

"You never knew any of her friends? You don't know anything about her?" Jack's words crackled as they snapped forcefully out of his mouth.

"Spoiled little witch like her mother. After her mother died, Patty ran off."

"Gee. Wonder why?" Replacement's arms went up and out in mock amazement.

"Shut your hole, you—"

Jack lunged forward and grabbed the arms of the chair. His face was inches away from the man who now leaned back, terrified. "Do you know anything, old man?"

"No. No." He shook his head.

"You don't get the other fifty," Jack spat. He shoved the chair and started to walk out.

"Wait. I got some of her stuff. It's in her bedroom. Down the hall. You can take a look for fifty."

Jack peered down the dark hallway. A worn brown carpet ran straight back to a door. Two other doors were halfway down.

"On the left," Mr. Cole called out.

"Stay there," Jack growled and took Replacement by the hand. "Stay near me."

"Are you kidding? I want to climb on your back."

Jack stood to the side of the door and pushed it open. The hinges groaned in protest. A small bedframe with no mattress sat against the far wall. Old plywood leaned against another corner, and trash littered the floor. Two sawhorses and old paint cans were stacked against the closest wall. It was still obvious it had once been a girl's bedroom. Yellowed posters of musicians and actors Jack didn't know clung to the walls.

Jack moved to the bureau, with Replacement following close behind. Faded stickers covered the front, but it was filled with old tools. Every drawer was empty of anything that would help them.

The closet was another story. The door had been removed and was leaning at an angle against the back of the closet. Jack picked it up and set it next to the plywood stack. Two cardboard boxes lay inside. They weren't sealed, but their covers were folded to keep them closed. Jack opened the first, and he could see stuffed animals. The second one had schoolbooks at the top. Quickly, he closed the boxes back up.

"This one is the lightest." He handed it to Replacement. "Head straight for the car."

"We can't just take it."

"Yes, I can."

Jack grabbed the other box and headed out of the room. He set it down when he got to the living room.

The old man stood in the middle of the room. "Don't bring that shi—"

"Shut up."

Jack held the door open, and Replacement walked past him with her box.

"You can't take anything."

Jack stayed in the house and shut the door after Replacement went through.

Darkness and silence descended on the little room. The old man took a step away from Jack.

Slowly, Jack's head rose up, and the old man gasped. "Fine. Just take it. Take it." His trembling hand pointed at the box.

Jack walked forward. "Do you know what you did to her? People said she was a good kid. You started it. What you did to her—"

"That's a lie." The old man stuck a bony hand out toward Jack.

"You're the one who's lying." Jack continued forward.

The old man sat down. "So?"

Jack stopped.

"So what if I did?" he spat. "The statute of limitations is long gone. No one believed it then, either. It doesn't matter anyway. I'm as good as dead. I got liver cancer. Doctors tell me I got a month or two. They want me in hospice. Do you think I'm scared of going to jail?"

Jack leaned down.

"You're not going to jail, old man, and I'm not going to kill you…today. I'm going to come back, though. I'm going to come back on Patty's special day. Do you remember what day that is? Do you remember how she loved that day every year? I'll come back on Patty's special day. When I do, I'm going to take a piece of you for her."

Jack threw the other fifty on the floor. When he turned around, Replacement stood in the doorway. He grabbed the other box and walked out.

"Jack?" Replacement hurried to keep up with him.

He tried to breathe deeply and get the stench out of his mouth and nose.

"What?" He popped the trunk and tossed the boxes in.

"What you just did. Back there? What's the special day mean?"

Jack ripped open the door and slid behind the wheel. After she got in, they flew down the road.

"Do you really think I'm going to come back and cut off a piece of him?"

"The way you just looked? Yes. That's a definite possibility."

"I won't. But he doesn't know that."

"He could call the cops."

"I am a cop." Jack flashed a big smile that wasn't returned. "Besides, he won't. He's a scumbag. Scumbags don't call the cops when they get threatened. It will take awhile to take hold anyway."

"What will?"

"What I said. Did you see the way he smiled when he thought his own daughter was dead but may have left him some money? I wanted him to hurt. I wanted him to remember Patty." Jack kept pushing the gas pedal down. "He didn't even remember her name right away. He didn't know anything about her. He won't remember any special day. But he thinks that's when I'm coming back. He'll lie awake at night, trying to remember. He'll go over every conversation that he ever had with Patty. I hope it drives him crazy, trying to figure out when it is. I hope it causes him to remember her. I hope it causes him lots of pain."

CHAPTER 26

Just Wondering

Jack and Replacement munched on fresh sandwiches they picked up at a country store they came across along the side of the road. Now they were waiting outside Jeff Franklin's apartment building.

"Do you think he knows anything?" Replacement asked.

"He wrote all the articles. Sometimes reporters get information that they can't print but it's still good information."

A small, blue, electric car finally rounded the bend and parked in front of the two-story building. Jack and Replacement hopped out of their car. The reporter shut the door and stared in their direction as they approached.

He was a small, thin man, almost the same size as Replacement. His head was bald on top and gray on the sides. Judging by his round glasses, white T-shirt, jeans, and open blue blazer, Jack would have guessed that he was a college professor.

"Can I help you?"

"I hope so. My name is Jack Stratton, and I need to ask you a few questions."

Jeff smiled. "I'm the one who usually says that." He laughed as he rushed over and shook their hands. "Your girlfriend?"

Jack shook his head. "This is Alice. I was wondering—"

"Please, come on in. We might as well be comfortable."

Jeff moved behind them so he could rush them down the brick walkway and inside the first apartment, which was his. The apartment was a brightly lit, extremely clean, open-plan layout. Light tan carpeting stretched everywhere, and a tiled kitchen was in the back.

"Please." He held his hands out and gestured to the couch. "What do you want to know?"

"I'm doing some research about the Steven Ritter case."

"Steven Ritter. The boy killed at Buckmaster? Are you a writer?"

"I'm interested in the case. It's more of a personal pursuit."

"Oh, you're a crime enthusiast. My sister is too. Her focus is the Long River Killer. She went out to Boulder, too." Jeff walked into the kitchen and gathered glasses. "I wrote most of the main articles on the Steven Ritter case. It was never solved. Shame, really. I'm mostly retired now."

"Did you personally talk to the people involved?"

He returned, carrying three glasses and a pitcher. "I interviewed everyone. Most twice. It was the biggest story the town ever had. Iced tea?"

"Yes, please." Replacement leaned forward. "Did anyone stand out?"

"No." He shrugged. "There was extremely little information on that case."

"I read all of your articles," Jack said and Jeff smiled broadly. "And I just had a couple of questions. What's your personal view of the case?"

Jeff took a sip of his iced tea. He nodded his head as if he was thinking about the question but Jack got the feeling that Jeff had long ago came to a conclusion about the case and was dying to share it. "Well, Steven Ritter was a Boy Scout. Literally." He turned his hands out. "No dirt on him. No enemies. Believe me, I turned over every rock. Zilch. It's a true mystery. No enemies and no one saw anything."

"There was never a suspect?"

"None. The police never came up with anyone and I knew Chief Wilson personally. He worked that case like it was his own son who'd been killed. He would have solved it, too. I think he was getting close before he died."

"When did he die?"

"Oh, three months after the murder. He had a heart attack at home. Mable, his wife, thought that case killed him. I'd have to agree. It really changed him."

Jack sat back on the couch and sighed. "Ripples in the pond," Jack muttered.

"Excuse me?"

"You don't think about the toll on other people." Jack rubbed his hand on his leg. "One event, but far-reaching effects."

Replacement tapped her glass. "Did you ever interview a Terry?"

Jack cringed.

Jeff looked at Replacement and squinted. "I don't remember. Where did you get the Terry tip?"

"It's not a tip." Jack set down his glass, wary about divulging any information.

"Are you two looking into the case? Did something similar happen in another town? A copycat?"

"No. No." Jack shook his head. "It's just research. Is there anything else you can tell us? Anyone you know who might have some more information?"

"Henry Cooper. He's still around."

"He was the first officer on the scene," Jack said.

"You did do your homework." Jeff gave Jack a reappraising gaze. "Henry found Steven. He might not be talkative."

"Why would that be?"

"Henry Cooper? The Peterson drowning? Father and son on a snowmobile?"

Jack looked at Replacement and they both shook their heads that they weren't familiar with it.

"Big news around here. Brian and Jarred Peterson were snowmobiling on Houtt's Pond. Their snowmobile went through the ice. Cooper was the first cop on the scene. He managed to save the boy, but Brian, the father, died. The problem was Cooper started talking to a TV reporter right after it happened. She smelled the whiskey on his breath. Chief had to fire him."

"Which chief?" Replacement put her head in her hand.

"Nelson."

"Nelson?" Jack repeated, confused. "He's a lieutenant."

"Now he is. The police chief is elected here. Every six years. Nelson was chief for sixteen years until he lost to Dennis."

"And Nelson stayed on the force?"

Jeff shrugged. "I found it kind of odd too. You'd think he'd retire. Now he has almost thirty years. He worked the Ritter case too."

"Did you find anything that you didn't print?"

"Well," he swirled his glass and stared down, "it was just a rumor of a rumor. I didn't feel right printing it." He looked out the window. "Everything about that kid was squeaky clean, but I did hear that Steven may have been 'involved' with a shady girl."

"Do you have a name?"

"Patricia Cole. She had a reputation of being the town trollop."

Replacement blurted out, "Patty Cole is Jack's mother." But the warning came a second too late.

The reporter looked as though he'd suddenly messed his pants. His eyes went wide, and his hand trembled as he brushed his remaining gray hair. "My apologies, sir. I had no idea…"

Jack's tone was ice-cold. "Your articles stopped so suddenly. Why?"

"I wasn't getting anywhere," Jeff continued. "There wasn't any new information. I tried to keep the story going, but it just faded."

Jack handed him a card. "Well, thank you for your time, sir."

"You didn't mention why you're looking into this. Can you elaborate?"

"It's…"

"We're doing some research for a family tree." Replacement smiled.

Jeff showed them to the door and they headed for the car.

Jack started the Impala. The engine hesitated briefly before it fired up. He turned his head to listen to the engine. After a few seconds, he patted the dashboard and backed out.

"Why do you do that?" Replacement asked.

"Do what?"

"Rub the car." She made a face.

"I didn't rub the car." He scowled back.

"You did. I just saw you."

"I patted it."

"It wasn't a pat. It was a rub."

"I'm not, like, caressing the car."

"Looked like it to me."

"Guys do that. She's my baby and she sounded off. I got worried."

Replacement's head wobbled back and forth. "I can't believe I'm jealous of a car." Her face suddenly turned beet red and she shifted to look out the window.

Jack drummed his thumbs against the steering wheel. "Can you look up Henry Cooper's address?"

"Sure."

Ten minutes later, they pulled into downtown. Cooper's address was listed as 43B Westmoore. Jack parked in front of the laundromat and looked up to the second floor.

"Those could be apartments." Replacement craned her neck to try to see.

"Let's check out back for a staircase."

The two people waiting in the laundromat watched them as they walked by. A small side road led behind the building. A worn wooden staircase badly in need of paint led up to two doors.

Wood creaked and Replacement held the rickety railing as they walked up. On the side of the doorframe, written in permanent marker, was a large 43B.

Jack motioned for Replacement to stay to the side while he knocked on the door. After a second, it yanked open. The guy was dressed in blue jeans, work boots, and a dirty sweatshirt.

"Henry Cooper?" Jack held out his hand. "I'm Jack Stratton. Can I have a couple minutes of your time?"

Henry's gray hair was cut short, and his face was deeply lined, but Jack guessed he was in his early fifties. He stood there, staring. One hand held onto the doorframe; the other he wiped on his pant leg before he shook Jack's hand. "Come on in." He held the door open and stepped aside.

Jack hesitated. He shot Replacement a quick sideways glance and walked in. The apartment was small. The first room was a dirty kitchen with a round table. Old, stick-on linoleum squares that looked to be excess from the laundromat below covered the floor.

Where the tiles ended, a worn carpet covered the living room floor. A couch, folding metal chair, and a medium-sized TV were the only furniture.

"You're his son." Henry picked up some papers from the kitchen chairs and put them on the counters. "Damn. You could be him."

Replacement sat down but Jack remained standing. "How did you know?"

"Small town. I'm a friend of Terry Bradford's."

The muscles in Jack's jaw flexed at the name.

"He's hard to take but he's a good guy. He didn't know you were Patty's kid." Henry sat down and put his hands on the table. "Are you really looking into it?"

Jack pulled out the chair and sat down. "I am. That's why I wanted to speak with you. You were the first officer on the scene?"

Henry's left hand trembled constantly. He grabbed it with his right. "Yeah. You're a cop, right?"

Jack hesitated.

"I heard," Henry continued. "Like I said, small town."

"Was he...was he alive when you got there?"

Henry shook his head. "No. The EMTs came right after me but there was nothing they could do."

"He never regained consciousness?"

Henry rubbed the back of his left knuckle with his right hand. "No. It was bad. The bastard who killed your father stabbed him a lot. They call it a rage killing. A lot of hate. Didn't make sense. Still doesn't make sense. I bet you can't find someone who hated that kid, even now."

"The paper said Frank Nelson handled most of the investigation—"

"That's why you don't trust those scumbags." Henry pressed his hands down on the table. "Nelson couldn't tie his own shoes. Guy was a moron and still is a moron. Chief ran the investigation. Nelson took it over after the chief died. You ask me, that's why they never caught the guy."

"You never had a suspect?"

"Nope. Your old man was a good kid. Well liked. No enemies."

"Did you know him?"

Henry crossed his arms and leaned back. "Yeah. Scouts. The chief was scout master and Nelson and I were assistants. I liked your dad. I don't think he liked me much. None of the kids really did." He scoffed. "I was just out of the Marines and was a little hard on them. Kids need that. Most of the other kids were little sissies, but your dad was a tough kid. A good kid."

"You never found the murder weapon?"

"Nah. By the time the state police could bring out a dive team, the pond froze. Nelson had us drag the lake come spring. But there were way too many lily pads. I figure the killer just took the knife with them. You want a drink?"

"Water." Jack took out a notebook. "I appreciate the answers. It helps me if I jot stuff down. Do you mind if we start at the beginning?"

Henry took down three glasses. "I got no other plans."

For the next two hours, Jack walked through everything that happened after Henry got to the pond. He added to his notes on everyone involved in the investigation and what they did.

When Jack finally closed the book and stood up, Henry remained sitting. He looked up at Jack with tired eyes. "Can I ask you a question?"

Jack hesitated at the door. "Ask."

"Did, ah, Patty tell you to talk to me?"

"No. How did you know Patty?"

Henry held up his hands and leaned back in his chair. "I didn't. I was just…thinking. You know, if she was a kid hanging out at the pond I might have busted her or something." He cleared his throat. "I was just curious why you'd come talk to me."

"Because you were the responding officer." Jack tried to maintain a neutral expression but he felt the muscles in his face harden with suspicion.

Henry nodded. "Yeah. That makes sense. I was just wondering."

Jack held the door for Replacement. As he went down the wobbly staircase, Jack started wondering too.

CHAPTER 27

Bad Gas

The Impala's engine sputtered as Jack turned the key. He grimaced and pumped the gas until it finally started.

"I'll have to go get some dry gas." Jack frowned as he pulled away from the curb.

"How can gas be dry?" Replacement looked at him oddly.

"It's just called dry. It's something you mix with your gas if you get water in the tank. The Impala just sounds rough."

Jack took a right onto the main street. His eyes shifted to the rearview mirror. An old, white pickup truck took the right too.

"Where are we going now?" Replacement asked.

Jack took another right, drove halfway down the street and pulled over to the curb. "Put your seat belt on."

"Okay…." Replacement made a face. "What's up?"

The truck pulled onto the street and came to a stop in the middle of the road.

"We've got a tail."

The driver of the pickup threw the truck into reverse and backed up to the main road.

Jack punched it and cut the wheel. Smoke billowed from the Impala's tires.

Replacement pressed against the door and then back into the seat as the car shot forward.

The pickup raced down Main Street and took a hard left.

Jack flew through the intersection after the car.

"Use your phone." Jack said as they slid into the turn. "Get the plate."

Replacement fumbled for her pocket as Jack tapped the brakes and then powered into the turn.

"We're in downtown," Replacement cautioned.

"I know. I got it."

The truck's brake light flashed at the end of the next road. The right light was out. The street was deserted.

Jack jammed the gas to the floor.

The Impala jerked forward.

"What the hell? No, baby. Come on."

The engine sputtered and died.

Jack slammed on the brakes, threw the transmission into park and tried to start the engine. The motor still turned over but the car wouldn't start.

Jack screamed in rage. A string of obscenities poured out of his mouth as he stared at the now deserted street.

"Tell me you got a plate."

Replacement grimaced. "No. Too far and the plate was too dirty."

Damn.

He turned the key again and the engine just sputtered.

Jack opened the door. "I'm going to try to get her going. When I tell you, give her some gas."

Replacement slid over into the driver's seat. Jack fiddled with the carburetor for twenty minutes but the car wouldn't keep running. Replacement smiled sheepishly. "Do you want me to call the garage?"

They had to wait another twenty minutes for the tow truck. The kid driving it was Replacement's age, and he was only a couple inches taller than she was. It took him only a few minutes to have the Impala hooked onto the back of the tow truck.

Jack and Replacement rode in the cab the five miles to the garage. The small building was a combination gas station, used car lot, and service station. One look at it and Jack was sure it was the same as it had been thirty years ago.

"What's the mechanic's name?" Jack asked the tow driver as he hopped out and helped Replacement down.

"Marty. He's my dad. I'm Matty." Matty flashed a quick smile. "I'll back your car right in, okay?"

"Thanks," Jack muttered as he headed into the garage. A man in his early forties, who looked like an older version of Matty, walked out the front door.

"You the fella who broke down on West Street?"

Jack nodded. "It just stalled. It was running fine, but this morning it sounded rough."

"When you get gas last?"

"Yesterday. And I got the gas here." Jack pointed toward the pumps.

"Then it's not the gas." Marty laughed. He looked at his watch and continued, "I have an inspection and an oil change in front of you. You want to check back in the morning?"

Replacement stepped forward. "We're on vacation, so the sooner you could get to it, the more we'd appreciate it."

Marty nodded. "I understand. I should be able to get started tonight but most likely it'll be morning. I can get you set up with a rental." He nodded to a car sitting outside. "It's great on gas, and you can have her for a few days. It's a little small."

Replacement looked at the little blue Volkswagen Beetle and pressed her hands together. "It's so cute!" She turned hopefully toward Jack.

Fifteen minutes later, Jack and Replacement walked back out of the office.

"I just have to grab something out of the trunk," Jack said.

Jack went over to the Impala, took out the two boxes that they got from Patty's house, and put them in the Volkswagen. "Do you want to drive?" He held up the keys.

"Yes!" Replacement beamed as she dashed over to the driver's side.

Jack had to put his seat almost all the way back to fit in.

Replacement was practically dancing in the seat as she adjusted the mirrors.

"This sucks," Jack muttered.

Replacement froze. "I'm sorry about your car."

"Me, too. Let's go back to the hotel and look this stuff over."

Replacement looked back at the boxes. "I wonder what's in there."

Once they reached the hotel, Jack and Replacement quickly headed upstairs to go through the boxes from the Cole house. The first box was filled with mementos that should have been displayed on a shelf: old stuffed animals, a trophy from an elementary spelling bee, and another one from gymnastics. A picture frame surrounded by hearts held a picture of Patty when she was only five or six, hugging a slender, smiling woman.

My other grandmother.

The woman looked a little like his mother, but she had a rounder face. Her smile was broad. They both looked quite happy. The glass in the frame was gone, but Jack could see small broken shards on the edge that still clung to the wood. The other box had two high school math books on top. Underneath was a stack of teen magazines from thirty years ago. At the bottom was a yearbook. Replacement lifted it out, puzzled.

"It's from middle school." She opened the old yearbook. It was small and yellowed with age. The front had water spots, and it smelled of mildew as she opened it. Replacement's nose crinkled. "How about we look at this…not on my bed?"

She scooted off and went to the desk. Jack moved to look over her shoulder. They found twelve pictures of Patty and two of Steven. In every picture, she was beaming.

"She looks like a happy kid," Jack muttered.

"I feel bad for her." Replacement didn't look at Jack.

She was a happy kid before her mother died and her father…

Replacement flipped to the back and, pressed between the pages, was a homemade card. She carefully lifted out the red construction paper valentine. It was in the shape of a heart with three arrows going through it from left to right. "Three arrows—that's a lot of love." Replacement slapped her leg. "PC & DJ. That's sweet. If she kept it, it was special to her."

"DJ?" Jack looked around. "Do you have the other yearbooks?"

"This is from middle school, Jack."

"We'll rule it out then." Jack grabbed a high school yearbook and flipped to the Js.

"You, too." He waved his hand at her yearbook.

After a few minutes, they both closed their books.

"Zip," Jack said.

"Nada. No names that start with *D* and end in *J*."

"Are you hungry?"

"I'm starving." She jumped up, went to the closet and took out the brown dress. "Can we go out? There's a little Italian place around the corner."

Inside, Jack groaned. The last thing he wanted to do was be at a crowded restaurant but the longer she looked at him, the bigger her green eyes became. Besides, he knew why she wanted to go.

"Sure."

Her face lit up and she danced into the bathroom, clutching the fawn-brown dress to her chest.

CHAPTER 28
What Are You Selling?

Jack smiled as he breathed in, and the scent of lilac drifted up. He could feel the warmth of breath against his cheek. He turned his head, and Replacement's face was right next to his. She lay cradled in his arms, still asleep. Her arm was around his waist, and her breath came in little puffs against his face. He froze.

Alice... You're easy to talk to. You're real. Genuine.

The fresh spring scent of the bedding mingled with the scent of her hair. She moaned softly, and her chin rose. Their lips were now only a breath apart. All Jack had to do was angle his head.

Oh man. Don't. Don't.

Jack tried not to breathe as he scooted backward and out of the bed.

Damn it.

Jack turned and almost ran for the bathroom.

Seriously, stupid, don't do it. I'm the only friend she has. If it didn't work out...

Jack washed his face and changed. He wrote a quick note letting her know he was going for a drive and put it on the pillow. Silently he gathered up his shoes, wallet, and keys, and slipped out the door.

Go for a ride. Think.

The inn was deserted as he headed down the staircase and out the door. The chill from the crisp air was refreshing. He breathed in deeply. The first rays of the morning lightened the sky, and a mist clung to the trees and ground.

Jack swung his arms and jogged for the car. It was the type of morning that made you want to run. The gravel crunched under his feet, but all around him was still. He paused at the small blue Bug. It was perfect for Replacement but he wanted his Impala back.

The little town was asleep as he pulled out and sped through the streets. He tried to remember whether there was a coffee shop near the inn but couldn't think of any.

Might as well get this over with.

Jack knew where he should go but he didn't want to go there. Not today. Never. He headed for Buckmaster Pond.

Get your mind back on track, Jack. Think. Facts. Patty asked to meet him. He heads there. Terry put her up to it, so...would he have picked up on that? Was he paranoid like me, or did he blindly rush out there?

The reset trip lever in the Bug resisted as Jack tried to press it, but it clicked and the miles finally read zero. He kept his head on a swivel as he drove out there.

What was he thinking? What would I do if I was a seventeen-year-old boy and my girlfriend calls me to meet her at night? Hell, I'd run out there, peeling my clothes off on the way.

The route to the pond took Jack on an almost straight run.

There are no businesses out here. Huge spots with no homes. Some look new, so there would have been even fewer out here then.

A half a mile from the pond, a little auxiliary fire station stood set back from the road. The lights were off and the driveway was empty.

Jack passed the last house before the turnoff to the pond. The fog was dense near the water, and it clung to the base of the pines.

A mile and a quarter here. It's an easy walk. Police report said he didn't take his bike.

Jack pulled into the pond parking lot. Sitting up as high in the seat as he could, he still couldn't see the water in the pond. As he stepped out of the car, he dug his hands into his pockets, and his left hand pressed against his gun. Shivering, he jogged down the little path. The large rock he saw in the crime-scene photos came into view. Jack slowed and then stopped.

The trees were larger but he was sure that this was the place.

It's the spot where my father died.

Jack exhaled. His breath came out in a puff and he watched it slowly dissipate.

There was a large log here. Patty said she came back. She must have called 911... No. There was no 911 then... The hair on the back of Jack's neck rose. *No 911 and no cell phones. Where would she have called from?*

Jack looked around. The last house he passed on the way here was half a mile away, but across the pond he could see a little house with its lights on. Jack jogged to a granite rock that went out over the water. From there, you could clearly see the small home.

She'd have gone there.

He started to jog as he also pulled out his cell phone. 8:30.

My mom would kill me for even thinking of knocking on someone's door this early but their lights are on. Someone's up.

Jack kept running until he reached the backyard of the little house. A manicured lawn led up to a small white cottage. Jack could see the kitchen light on. Staying to the edge of the lawn, he made his way around the front. He walked up the stone walk and exhaled before he knocked on the black front door. He looked out onto the empty street and back to his feet.

He was about to give up when someone opened the door.

A middle-aged woman in sweatpants and a T-shirt smiled broadly as she looked Jack up and down with a widening grin. "Hello." She leaned against the doorframe.

"Hi. My name is Jack Stratton, and I was wondering if I might ask you a couple of questions."

"I'd love to help you out but what're you selling?"

Jack swallowed and shifted his weight. "Nothing. I'm not a salesman. Actually, I had a question, but you're far too young to have lived here twenty-six years ago."

"Honey, I like the way you talk." She grinned from ear to ear and shook her mane of red hair. "I hate to admit it, but yeah, I did live here then. I'd have been, like, nine."

"Who's there?" a woman called from inside.

"It's fine, Mom. There's a young man asking for directions."

"Shut the door or invite him in. It's freezing."

"Your clock is ticking." The redhead winked. "Ask away."

"Do you remember the night when Steven Ritter was killed?"

The woman's face went white, and the smile vanished. She cleared her throat. "The boy at the pond? I was little. I don't know anything about it beyond that." Her hand moved to the doorknob.

"Did a girl come here that night and use your phone?"

Her eyes went wide and her neck lengthened. A second later, she shook her head. "No," she blurted out. "Nothing like that happened that night. I'm sorry but I need to go."

"Abbey? Abbey, shut the door." An old woman walked into the hallway. When she noticed Jack, she stopped, pulled her large robe tightly around herself, and a hand went to her curled hair.

"Please. I need to know. Steven Ritter was my father."

The old woman stood there and stared at him. Jack could see the debate raging inside her—whether to talk to him or not. He turned his palms out and slightly lowered his head. "Please."

"Let him in, Abbey," she whispered.

Abbey stepped aside and looked down at the floor.

"Thank you." Jack kept his head slightly down as he entered.

The inside of the house looked as if it would be better suited to Florida with its tan tile floor and white walls. The back of the house immediately caught Jack's attention. The whole rear wall was glass and looked directly across the pond.

"Do you want a coffee?" The old woman shuffled into a kitchen to the right and sat down. "That one has cream and sugar." She pointed to a cup on the table. "I put it out for Abbey, but she hasn't touched it yet."

"Thank you." Jack sat down.

"Who are you?"

"My name is Jack Stratton. Steven Ritter was my father."

The woman reached out for her coffee cup, but her hands trembled so she quickly put them back in her lap.

"You were home that night?" Jack asked.

The old woman nodded.

"Did a young girl come here and make a phone call?"

Abbey and her mother exchanged a quick glance, and the old woman shook her head. "No."

"Ma'am, I know Patricia Cole called the police from here that night."

The old woman looked down and then glared back at Jack. "I'm sorry about your father, but don't go calling me a liar."

"You are lying. Patty is my mother." Jack let the words hang.

The woman slumped in her chair. "Oh, son. I'm so sorry." She looked closer at Jack and leaned back again. "Oh, dear Lord. Patty and Steven?" Tears welled up in her eyes. "I'm Patty's godmother." She closed her eyes for a moment. "Patty's mother was my best friend. I promised her that I'd look after Patty."

"Can you please tell me what happened? Start with the first thing you remember."

"Patty showed up that night, covered in blood and pounding on the door. I just about went out of my mind. She was screaming that someone was stabbed. She didn't have anything to do with it. I just know it."

"How?"

"What?"

"How do you know she had nothing to do with it?"

The old woman looked at Jack as if he had four heads. "She's your mother. Don't you know your mother better than that?"

Jack closed his eyes. "No, I don't. Last week, I saw her for the first time in almost twenty years."

Abbey sat down.

"I'm just looking for answers. When Patty came to the door, was anyone with her? Did you see or hear a car?"

"No. She was alone. She kept saying he was hurt. She called the fire department for an ambulance."

"She called?"

The woman nodded again. "Patty was hysterical. The EMTs rushed right out. We watched until they left, but the police stayed a long time. Too long. I knew it was bad because of that."

"Why didn't you go to the police?"

"To report what? That Patty found a stabbed boy? They'd think she had something to do with it. I knew she didn't. Deep down, Patty was a good girl. She just found Steven that way. Besides, Patty's father was a bastard. A meaner man never lived. I don't know what he'd have done to her."

"What happened after?"

"I drove her home. I made her swear never to talk about it. But, Patty ran away a couple of months later. I haven't seen her since. Is she okay?"

Jack ignored the question. "Can you please try to remember if she said anything. Anything at all."

"She didn't."

"Did she mention any names?"

"No." She pulled her robe tight. "She didn't have anything to do with it. I know it. I knew Patty since she was a little girl, but if I thought she had anything to do with it or knew something, I'd have had her talk to the police."

Jack stood up. The old woman remained sitting but reached out and grabbed his wrist.

"Can you tell her that I hope she's well?"

Jack's head spun. *The old woman thinks she did the right thing but if Patty had only gone to the police, she may have gotten the help she needed.* He nodded. "Thanks for the coffee," he muttered and headed for the door.

Jack paused in the hallway as he looked back across the pond.

Abbey walked ahead of him and opened the front door.

"Thank you for your time." Jack nodded as he passed her.

"I'm sorry about your dad. I didn't know him, but I liked Patty. She was always real nice to me."

"Did you see anything that night?"

Abbey shook her head. "I saw the emergency lights at the pond that night, but when Patty came later, my mom made me go to bed."

"Thanks." Jack reached into his pocket and took out one of his cards.

"If you can remember anything else, please give me a call."

"I will. I'm sorry for your loss."

As he walked down the path, Jack's steps slowed.

The sunlight gleamed on the water of the pond. Jack gazed across to the shore on the other side. A hawk rose up out of the trees. It rose high overhead and then swooped low as it flew along the bank.

The morning was beautiful but Jack felt like a shadow passed over his soul. Something felt wrong. Something felt bad.

Jack looked at the darkened path that he took to get here and he hesitated. Like a child afraid of the woods, he stood with his hands thrust deep in his pockets and stared down the trail.

The warning of the little girl in his dream echoed somewhere in his mind.

Jack was afraid. But Jack didn't handle fear the way most people did. He didn't look at fear the same either. He gave the fear a second to wash over him. He felt his heart sped up and he swallowed. To Jack, fear was an action.

Jack yanked his hands out of his pockets and marched forward.

And for every action, there is an equal and opposite reaction.

After a few steps, Jack broke into a run.

Some people chose to react to fear by running away. Not Jack. Jack always chose to run straight at fear and make fear, fear him.

CHAPTER 29

Two Choices

Jack jogged back around the pond. He was at the midway point, so he decided to keep going and complete the loop. The cool air on his face felt wonderful, and the rhythm of his feet on the path seemed to be urging him on. The pond's surface was absolutely still. He looked at the treetops, and no wind blew the branches. As he rounded the bend to the rocks, he slowed. He hopped up on the rock and looked out over the pond. The water was crystal-clear. He peered over the side and could see at least fifteen feet down, but the bottom was still murky.

A familiar streak of air whizzed by his head, followed by a distant, loud crack. From years in the army, Jack's body reacted instantly. He leapt forward and landed on his belly. Rolling left, he scrambled behind a rock. Another shot whooshed overhead, followed by another distant crack.

Shot came from the parking lot.

Jack's gun was in his hand. He was lying on his stomach with the rock between him and the shooter. Jack checked his gun. A rifle versus a pistol—he'd knew he'd lose. He had two choices: run away or flank.

He looked at the slope of the ground and the small gully that could provide cover. He'd be exposed while he crossed the path, but the trees would help obscure him. He sprinted to the left, staying low, and slid to a stop behind a large pine.

Nothing. No shot.

A large oak was twenty yards away. Forcing himself, he exhaled slowly to get his breathing under control. He dashed forward to his next point of shelter, pressed his back against the rough bark, and listened.

Nothing. Damn. Now I don't know where they are. Are they rabbiting or lining up a clear shot?

In the distance, he heard a car engine. Jack broke into a full run. Through the trees, he could barely make out the parking lot when he caught a flash of reverse lights as a car pulled out. His muscles strained, and his legs burned, but he sprinted as fast as he could for the road. Branches tore at his face and clothes, but he pushed on. Bursting out of the woods, he stumbled yet remained on his feet. The fleeing car was already out of sight. He debated about running for the Bug, but the shooter's car was long gone.

Jack screamed at the sky.

CHAPTER 30

Just a Fish

Jack felt a mix of relief and frustration as he walked back to the parking lot. The echo of the gunshot in his mind made his skin feel cold. He'd been a stationary target. The familiar question every soldier asks rushed back— *why didn't I die today?*

As Jack drove away from the pond, all he wanted to do was keep driving. He'd love to be able to take his police cruiser out, just open her up, and let her run. Instead, the hum of the Bug's little motor made him feel trapped. As he leaned back in the seat, he felt a slight tremble in his left leg.

No.

He gripped the steering wheel with one hand and frantically rolled down his window. The glass seemed to move in slow motion but Jack needed it open now. He needed to feel the wind.

Please, not now.

He pressed his face against the cold glass with desperation, as if the car were filling with water. He gritted his teeth and closed his eyes.

Jack!

His foot was jammed down on the gas. The Bug was blindly flying down the road, and he was just a passenger in a pilotless ship. Jack knew his eyes were closed, but he didn't know whether his body refused to obey him or whether his mind refused to give the command to stop.

He screamed and slammed his foot down on the brake. Everything not fastened down in the Bug flew forward. He could hear things fly off the dashboard. His body jerked into the seat belt and his chin jammed against his chest, but his eyes remained closed. The force of the deceleration had pushed him against the steering wheel. He sat there, panting into it. His body was rigid.

As grief overtook him, his body suddenly relaxed and slumped over the wheel, his hands now on the dash. His foot slipped off the brake, and the pedal came back up with a faint thump.

Jack opened his eyes.

The Bug was slowly rolling back into his lane, and the road was empty. Jack sat back up and steered the car, so it was mostly on the side of the road. His hand continued to shake as he shut the engine off.

You stupid idiot.

He pulled the rearview mirror over so he could glare at himself. He expected his own eyes to be filled with condemnation, hate even. As he stared at his reflection, he didn't see disgust at this weakness; instead, he saw concern.

I'm going to get someone else killed. What's wrong with me? I'm fine when someone shoots at me...I'm not afraid while I chase a guy with a gun, but afterward I freak out?

Jack looked up at the ceiling.

I can deal with it. I can...

He put his head in his hands and rubbed his face.

Please, God... Please, God help me.

A little while later, Jack pulled into the inn parking lot just as the chief's Crown Vic rolled in. Both men got out of their cars.

"You sure know how to get people riled up." Dennis walked over. "I was having breakfast and nearly choked when I opened my paper." Dennis handed Jack a newspaper.

He opened it up to the headline: "Hunting for His Father's Killer— Policeman son has a new lead in the twenty-seven-year-old murder at Buckmaster Pond."

"Damn." Jack's mouth fell open.

"You can say that again, Jack." Dennis tapped the paper with his finger. "The son of Steven Ritter is set to break this cold case wide open with new information."

"Is this paper just local?"

"Yeah, why?"

"You have no idea what my boss is going to do if he sees this." Jack rubbed his head.

"I don't know what your boss will do but mine already called. Now the mayor wants me to let him know what new lead I found. The problem is, I don't have one. You got some new evidence, and you don't share it with me? I've got to read about it in the funny pages?"

"I never told that reporter I found anything new..." Jack's voice trailed off.

"You talked to a reporter? Real smart."

"It was off the record."

"Yeah, reporters always keep their word. What the hell did you tell him?"

"Nothing. I said I was doing family research."

"He's a reporter. A bottom feeder. Right up there with lawyers. Do you know the difference between a catfish and a reporter?"

"No."

"One is a scum-sucking bottom feeder, and the other is just a fish." Dennis laughed at his own joke. "Live and learn, boy. Live and learn. Never talk to them. Franklin said you had new information. What have you got?"

"I didn't tell him anything." Jack stalled. Someone had just shot at him, and now everything was blowing up. The fewer people who knew information right now, the better.

"Think, Jack. Did you say anything else? I need to solve this case too. I know he was your father, but Steven was my best friend. I don't know if you know what that's like, but there's not a day that goes by that I don't think about him. But every time I do, I remember that the bastard who killed him is still walking around, drawing breath. Every time I see his mother..." Dennis wiped his eyes. "My dad didn't live long enough to solve it, but I need to. For both of them."

Replacement bounded out of the inn and down the steps.

Dennis waved and then turned to Jack. "I'm going to go talk to Franklin but he always pulls that reporter confidentiality crap. You let me know if you find something." He waved to Replacement again as he got into his car.

Replacement rushed over to Jack. "Let's talk in the car," she whispered as she waved and smiled at Dennis.

They got in the Bug and Replacement swiveled to face him. "This is a problem." She opened the newspaper. "Franklin's writing another article. He plans on laying it all out."

"There's nothing to lay out. It's not a big deal. It's a local paper."

"Well, it freaked me out when I saw it. Where were you this morning?"

"I wanted to go out to the pond. Then...I went for a run."

"You look like you went for a roll. You're all muddy."

"Actually, I think the paper might have helped in a strange way, too."

"Why?"

Jack cleared his throat. He knew how protective Replacement was but he couldn't think of a way to ease into the fact that someone tried to kill him. "Someone took a shot at me out at the pond."

"They tried to punch you?" She laughed. "What a dope."

When Jack didn't return her smile, Replacement's eyes slowly widened. "You don't mean took a shot at you like shot like a gun?"

Jack gave her a it-could-a-been-worse grin. "They missed."

Replacement grabbed him by the jacket and frantically checked him over. "Are you okay?"

"I'm fine." Jack held her hands. "They missed. I chased after them but they got away."

Replacement sat there, staring at him. The longer she went without saying anything, the more nervous Jack became. She slowly gripped his hands tighter. "Are you trying to tell me that you *chased* a guy who had a gun and tried to kill you with it?"

"I have a gun, too."

"You risked your life."

"That's my job."

"Jack…"

He expected her to yell. To scold him and tell him he was foolhardy and irresponsible. He braced himself for her arguments and hastily prepared his mental rebuttals. But when she opened her mouth and her chin started to tremble, that caught him completely off guard.

"I'm fine." He opened his arms to show her and she shot forward.

Her arms wrapped around his waist. She pressed her face against his chest.

Jack held her and rubbed her back. He let his head rest against the top of her soft hair and closed his eyes. He felt his whole body relax. The memory of the gunshot faded further. He pulled her even closer as a sense of relief and comfort swept over him.

She made him feel good and it felt so long since he felt that way. He let himself go and relaxed into her.

A sudden tapping at the window made them both jump.

A tall woman dressed in a short miniskirt, and a tight, low-cut blouse tapped on the window with her car key.

"Kristine?" Jack's lip curled.

Replacement rolled down the window and Kristine's words rushed in. "He wants to meet now. At the Walmart. Before he goes to work. We go with the plan. You follow me."

Kristine turned on her four-inch heels and rushed to her car.

"Go. Go." Replacement put on her seat belt.

"Where? What plan?"

"Follow her." Replacement pointed. "Walmart."

Kristine zoomed out of the parking lot and Jack followed.

"Why is she going dressed like that?" Jack asked.

"She's undercover. Scary thing is," Replacement began, "she looks like your old girlfriend, Gina. Remember her? The crazy one? She's…hey, stop smiling."

"What?"

"Don't smile when I talk about an old girlfriend."

"What?"

"You should frown or something."

"I wasn't smiling about her. I was thinking about when you chased her out of the apartment. But hold on. What are you talking about and where—"

"Speed up! You're losing her." Replacement bounced in her seat.

Jack jammed the gas to the floor and the little engine whined in protest. "What is going on?"

Replacement's grin quickly vanished. "Well… You weren't here to ask and you didn't bring your phone."

Kristine's car took a hard left and a large SUV cut between Jack and her.

"Crud." Jack hit the brakes and threw his hands up.

"Don't lose her."

Jack sped back up but the SUV was now between them and Kristine.

The light ahead turned yellow. Kristine darted through the intersection. The SUV sped up and then braked hard at the lights.

Jack slammed on the brakes.

Replacement grabbed the roof handle.

They stopped inches away from the SUV's bumper.

Tires skidded behind them and Jack grimaced as he braced for possible impact. The sedan behind them stopped in time but the young driver's eyes were huge and his face was white.

"We're losing her!" Replacement thrust both her hands out.

Kristine's car had made it through the light, took a left and now disappeared down the road.

"Why doesn't she stop?" Jack's voice rose. "Call her. Call this whole thing off until you explain to me just what the hell is going on."

Replacement took out her phone and called Kristine. "Terry Watkins chatted this morning that he wanted to meet Patty, aka Kristine—today. I thought—"

"Seriously?" Jack laid on the horn.

The guy in the SUV flipped Jack off.

Jack threw his door open. "Pull forward—NOW," he ordered in a voice trained by the United States Army to give commands that would be obeyed.

The SUV pulled forward enough to let the Bug by. Jack zipped through the intersection.

The road Kristine turned down was now empty.

"She's not picking up her phone," Replacement said. Kristine's answering message clicked on and Replacement spoke. "Kristine, abort the plan. Jack wants to talk first."

"Use your GPS to find the Walmart. Now, what's this *plan*?"

"Kristine agreed to meet Terry *after* work. We figured that we could go over the plan with you by the time you got back. I thought we had plenty of time. But Terry must have changed the time."

"But what's the plan?"

"Kristine goes undercover as Patty!" Replacement said it as if it were the most obvious thing in the world.

"She doesn't look like Patty."

"She's close enough. Seriously—same height, blue eyes. Besides, it's been almost thirty years. He'll think she's Patty since I used Kristine's picture for her profile."

"So she meets him—then what?"

"That's where her cell phone is." Replacement smacked her forehead. "It's in the back of her car."

"Call her again then. Have you found the Walmart yet?"

"The signal out here blows. Finally!" Replacement looked back. "Crud. Walmart is behind us and to the right. Take the right up here."

Tires screeched as Jack flew into the turn.

Replacement's knuckles turned white on the ceiling handle.

"Do you two realize she's meeting a killer? This isn't a game. Call her again."

"She won't pick up."

"Call her."

Replacement huffed as she frantically pressed buttons. "She can't. We hid her phone in the back of the car to record his confession. Like an undercover camera. I'll try to connect to it now."

The steering wheel creaked as Jack tried to restrain himself from ripping it off. "You can't record them. It's not admissible. Do you have any idea how dangerous this is?"

Replacement's green eyes flamed. "Yes. I do. Kristine does, too. She loved Steven. She still feels responsible in a way. She wants to get the guy too. She's the one who came up with the plan. THERE!"

Jack sped up and turned in. Both of them frantically searched the parking spaces out front but Kristine's car was not there.

Jack headed around the building. He slowed at the corner. "Got it." Jack pointed at Kristine's car parked in the back corner of the lot. Next to it was a tan Audi. The Audi was empty and two people sat in Kristine's car.

Jack pulled next to a dumpster. His fingers drummed on the steering wheel. "I have to stop her. If Terry did have something to do with Steven's murder, this is way too dangerous."

"We're right here if something happens. You have to at least give her a minute. Wait. I almost got it." Replacement held out her phone. The screen flickered and the inside of Kristine's car appeared. "It's like a one-way chat but I can record it," Replacement explained as she turned up the volume.

"No. No, you look great, Patty." Terry sat in the passenger seat. "Wow. Really great."

"It's been a long time. I'm surprised you remembered me." Kristine was partly turned in the driver's seat to face Terry.

"Of course I remembered you. I just didn't expect you to reach out to me." He ogled her up and down. "Wow. I can't believe it's been almost thirty years. You wrote that you're still dancing? I mean, that's great. You still have the body for it."

Kristine cleared her throat and Jack felt the bile rise in his own as Terry leered at her chest.

"It pays the bills." Kristine nodded.

"What kind of dancer did Kristine say she was?" Jack asked.

Replacement looked up, puzzled. "What do you mean? Like a ballerina...a dancer's another way of saying she's a— Oh, you don't think that he thinks she's a stripper kind of dancer?"

"You know," Terry continued. "I was glad I could help you out before."

"In high school?" Kristine added.

Terry shifted uncomfortably. "Yes but I just wanted to help out. I always hoped that money gave you a fresh start, Patty."

"Well, you were who I turned to." Kristine nodded.

"And I'm glad that you did. Listen, I'm really glad that you're back in town. So, do you need some help again?" Terry leaned closer.

Jack felt his finger's tightening on the case of the phone.

Terry reached into his pocket and took out an envelope. "It's two hundred and fifty dollars. I figure that you'll return the same favor for it?"

Kristine leaned away.

"What?" Terry's voice went up. "I'm not paying more. I...wait a minute. I know you. You're not Patty."

Jack threw his door open and sprinted across the parking lot, with Replacement running after him.

"Jack, wait!" Replacement called out.

Jack ripped Kristine's door open and dragged Terry out.

"What the hell is this?" Terry's eyes darted from Kristine to Replacement and settled on Jack. "This is a mistake. I don't know her. I thought she was someone else."

"Shut your mouth, you low-life pervert," Jack growled.

"You're not the police." Terry backed up. "If this is one of the got-you sting shows…"

"It's not." Jack stepped forward. "But I am going to the police."

Terry's face went white and he looked as if he was about to throw up. His hands slowly started to rise. "Wait a second. You can't. I… Here." He held the envelope out. "Take it."

Jack smacked it away. "I don't want your money. Patty Cole's my mother."

"Patty's your mother?" Terry visibly shook now. "I helped her. I was her counselor."

"Helped her?" Jack spat the words. "Patty came to you. She was a child. I heard you. She asked for your help but what did you make her do for it?" Jack's voice was cold.

Terry took three strides backward. "You can't prove that. I'll deny everything. The police won't believe you."

"I bet your wife will," Replacement said.

"No." Terry thrust his thumb at his own chest. "She'll believe me."

"I bet your wife believes her own lying eyes." Replacement held up her phone. "I hope she takes you to the cleaners in the divorce."

Jack glared at Terry. "My mother came to you for help, and you used her. I should kill you right now."

Terry turned and ran.

Replacement grabbed Jack's arm. "He's not worth it."

"Damn it!" Kristine yelled and then leaned against the car. She buried her face in her hands. Her shoulders trembled and she began to cry. "It's my fault. He knew Patty but I couldn't get him to talk about Steven."

"He didn't kill Steven." Jack watched Terry run around the corner of the building. "Patty came to Terry after Steven was killed. She wanted to leave town. That's why she took the money."

Kristine pressed the heels of her hands against her face. "Then this is a dead end?"

Jack nodded.

Kristine hung her head. "Now what do we do?"

Jack turned back toward her. "We dig deeper."

CHAPTER 31

Warp Speed

Kristine's car pulled out of the parking lot and Jack followed.

"Why?" Jack's voice was low and hollow.

"What?" Replacement's hand touched his shoulder.

"Everyone Patty turned to treated her like garbage." Jack gritted his teeth. "She couldn't catch a break. Her scumbag father. People using her. Then she goes to her guidance counselor and…seriously? Do girls…?" Jack looked down at Replacement and noticed the hurt in her own eyes. *If I ever catch the guy who hurt you…*

After another mile, Kristine stopped at a red light. "Oh, snap!" Replacement took out her phone and frantically started to type.

"What now?"

"Mrs. Ritter. I totally forgot. I don't want her to read the paper."

"You're texting her?"

Replacement laughed. "No. There's no way she has a smartphone. I'm texting Kris."

"Who?"

"Kristine. She told me her friends call her, Kris. Did you know she stops by Mrs. Ritter's every week?"

The light turned green, but Jack didn't move.

"What? Jack?" Replacement looked around. "What's wrong?"

Jack didn't answer. He stared straight ahead. "No way," he muttered a second before he jammed the gas pedal to the floor. The Bug sprung forward so fast the whole frame shook. Replacement grabbed the handle at the ceiling. Drivers laid on their horns, and cars skidded to avoid the little Bug that now raced through the intersection.

"You're completely freaking me out."

"I have to get back to the inn."

"At warp speed?"

Jack quickly passed Kristine's car. Replacement looked out the passenger window and shrugged as they zoomed by. They flew through a stop sign. He veered into the other lane, and cars swerved to get out of the way. The car tilted to the left as he hit the next turn, and the rear end fishtailed. Jack pumped the brake and jammed the gas.

When they reached the inn parking lot, he slammed on the brakes and skidded into a spot. He bolted out of the car and sprinted for the inn.

"Jack! Jack!" Replacement called after him, but he kept running.

He raced up the front steps as he thundered up the inside staircase. The door to his room was propped open, and when he charged in, a young cleaning woman gasped.

"Sorry," he panted. "All set. Out you go. Thanks."

She scampered out of the room. Jack rushed to the desk and grabbed the yearbook. He scanned page after page.

Replacement reached the room, breathless. She leaned against the desk. "What's going on?"

Jack kept flipping through the yearbook, frantically searching the pages and looking through each picture.

"What are you looking for?"

"Kristine goes by Kris, right?" After he turned the last page, he flipped back. "Her—she's the only one. You said *her* name." Jack slammed the yearbook down and jammed his finger on the page.

"Theresa Cook?" Replacement stared at the picture of the attractive girl with big poufy hair and her eyes slowly widened as she read the girl's nickname below the caption. "Terri with an *i*."

Jack clenched his fists until they were both next to the side of his head. "Damn it, I thought she was talking about a boyfriend. I never thought…"

"Jack…we still don't know—"

"It's her."

"Slow up. Just because she's the only Terri doesn't—"

Kristine ran up the stairs. She was out of breath. "What happened?"

"Did you know a Theresa Cook?"

"The Cooks live over near the dump. I went to school with her brothers, Billy and Bobby. Twins."

"Was she friends with Patty?"

Kristine shrugged. "I don't know. They were the back-of-the-class types. They smoked and hung out near the dugouts."

"Do they still live there?"

"Yes. It's a large, white farmhouse—just take a left before the dump."

Jack stomped by her. Her keys were on the front counter.

"Wait. We'll all go," Replacement called after him.

As Jack turned around, he covertly picked up and palmed Kristine's keys. "No. You stay here."

"You can't go there. They're bad news," Kristine said. "Both of the Cooks have been in and out of jail."

Jack kept going.

"Alice? Alice, can you stop him?"

Replacement raced to catch him. "Wait, Jack."

Jack didn't slow. "You need to stay here."

Replacement followed him out to the car. Jack got in and locked the doors again before Replacement reached the car.

"Jack, don't do this." Replacement pulled vainly on the handle.

Jack started the Bug and backed up as Replacement turned and ran back to the inn.

CHAPTER 32

Beg

The Bug stopped in front of the old farmhouse. A cloud of dust caught up to it before slowly fading. Jack gripped the wheel and tried to slow his breathing, but he was still almost panting with fury.

Jack stepped out of the car and headed for the house. Three trucks and four cars were parked around the front: some on the semi-circular driveway, some on the grass. Jack scanned them. Most of them didn't look as if they were in working condition.

His eyes stopped on the old white pickup with the broken taillight. It was the truck that had followed him around town.

As Jack started up the three steps to the wide porch, he could see a man walk down a hallway carrying a large box.

Jack stopped on the top step.

The man was dressed in blue jeans, boots, and a tan work coat. He looked to be around Jack's age but he was a medium-built man, both in height and weight. The box covered his face, but as he turned to get out of the door, Jack could see his brown hair and bulldog-like features.

The man's smile faded as he stared at Jack, and he stood there, slack-jawed. He sucked in a long, deep breath, as his eyes grew large. The box he carried fell to the porch with a loud crash and unidentifiable pieces scattered across the porch in all directions.

"Leave!" The man pointed at Jack. "Leave now."

"You're the one who's been following me." Jack stepped forward. His foot crunched a piece of broken glass.

"Are you okay, Randy?" a woman called out from inside.

Randy glanced nervously over his shoulder. "Stay inside, Mom." When he looked back at Jack, he hung his head. "I'm sorry."

Jack grabbed him by the jacket, spun him around and slammed him into the side of the house. "You tried to kill me."

Randy went even whiter. "What? No."

The sound of a car skidding to a stop in the driveway made both men look. Kristine's car slid to a stop and Replacement and she jumped out.

Guess she had spare keys. Jack glared down at the man. He shook him by his jacket. "You shot at me."

"No. No." Randy held up his hands. "I don't have a gun."

"Jack!" Replacement called out as she ran up the steps.

Jack shook him so hard his teeth clacked. He roared like a demon set free. "You know who killed my father. WHERE IS HE?"

"They didn't kill him. They didn't." Randy shook his head.

"RANDY!" A woman screamed and ran out the front door and onto the porch. She got between Jack and Randy. "Please don't hurt him," she wailed as she pulled on Jack's arms.

Jack looked at her face again. It was the librarian—Mae.

Mae tugged on Jack's arms, but she might as well have been pulling against stone. "They didn't do it. They didn't kill him." She was crying hysterically.

"Jack, please." Replacement placed her hand on Jack's arm.

"Explain." Jack let Randy go.

"They didn't kill Steven." Mae turned to face Jack.

"You were there?"

Mae nodded. "We all were. Billy, Bobby, Terri, and me. But they didn't kill him."

"What happened?" Replacement's voice was steady.

"It was… We were all—" Mae tried to catch her breath. "My brother Bobby liked Patty but Patty liked Steven. So Terri tricked Patty to get Steven to go to the pond."

"She set him up." Jack's voice was a barely controlled snarl.

Mae nodded. "Yes. They all waited for him. I liked Steven." She started to cry again. "Patty didn't know. She didn't. Bobby confronted Steven at the fire pit. They got in a fight. Steven started winning…"

Jack's throat tightened. "So Billy jumped in too."

Mae didn't look at Jack but she nodded. "They beat him up pretty bad, but they didn't kill him. They didn't." Mae wept. "Steven was alive when we took off."

"You took off? Why?"

"Someone must have called about the fight. We saw emergency lights in the parking lot and ran."

Jack held up his hand. "What kind of lights? Police?"

"Maybe. I couldn't see the car, just the lights. They pulled into the parking lot." Mae wrung her hands. "So we all ran."

Jack closed his eyes, and his words were clipped. "Where are your brothers? Let them explain it to me."

"They moved to Reno. I haven't spoken to them in years."

"Where's Terri? Let her tell me."

"She can't," Randy answered. "She's dead. Breast cancer. Three years ago."

Mae grabbed Jack's arm. "I'm sorry. I'm so sorry."

Jack glared at Randy. "Why were you following me?"

"It's my fault," Mae said. "When you came to the library, I just knew who you were. I saw you looking at the microfiche of the murder. I panicked. I called Randy. He's my son."

Randy held both hands in front of himself. "I'm sorry. I'll pay for your car. I'll pay for the tires."

"You'll do more than that. You shot at me. You're both going to jail."

"What? No." Randy shook his head.

Mae covered her face and wept.

"I slashed your tires and put sugar in your tank but I was trying to scare you off. I didn't shoot at you. I don't own a gun. I swear I'll pay for the damage. But please. My mom had nothing to do with killing your father. She didn't know I was following you. I swear it on my father's grave."

Jack turned around and grabbed the railing of the porch. His chest felt as if an anvil had fallen on it. He walked down the steps and over to the Bug. Replacement and Kristine followed. He leaned against the car and then held onto the roof.

Replacement came up behind him, reached into his pocket, and took out the keys. He didn't protest as she opened the passenger door.

"Jack?"

He felt as though she called to him from far away.

Jack looked back at the house. Randy had his arm around Mae's shoulder as he led her back inside.

"They didn't do it." Jack hung his head.

"If they didn't do it, who did?" Kristine asked.

CHAPTER 33

Gracie

Jack, Replacement, and Kristine all stood in the room behind the front desk. Jack paced the floor.

Kristine held her teacup with both hands. "Are you certain they didn't kill Steven?"

Jack leaned against the doorframe with his arms crossed. "Yeah. A woman who lives across the pond confirmed it. She saw the emergency lights and a little while later, Patty showed up, asking to call the police. I thought she got the order of events screwed up because she was a kid then. But she was right. Steven was alive when the brothers left. They got in a fight but they ran when they saw the emergency lights."

"That only leaves two cops." Replacement paced the floor. "Henry Cooper and Frank Nelson."

"Neither of them said police lights. It could be police lights or it could've been an emergency vehicle. There's an auxiliary fire station right near the pond," Jack said. "We need to get a list of who was on duty that night."

Kristine stood up. "I know just the person to ask."

A half an hour later, Replacement pulled in front of the cute colonial set back from the road. A red Toyota sat in the driveway.

"Kristine said she called to ask if we could come over." Jack opened the door.

"She said Gracie is a friend of your grandmother's," Replacement said. "She was the emergency service dispatcher then."

"Perfect." Jack hurried up the walkway and knocked on the dark-brown door.

After a moment, an older man opened the door and smiled.

"Jack? Alice?" He reached out a hand and then motioned for them to come in. "I'm Thomas Hickoring. You're here to see my Gracie."

"Yes. Thank you, sir."

Jack let Replacement go in before him. He could smell cinnamon and apples cooking and, even though he wasn't hungry, his stomach growled. The house had bright wood floors and a staircase led off upstairs. A hallway ran straight back to a kitchen, and Thomas slowly led them to the family room to the right. He held open a glass-paned door that led into the carpeted room. An older woman sat on a loveseat, with her hands folded in her lap. She had on a plain blue dress, and her leg was propped up on a footstool.

"Come in." The woman beckoned them with both hands. "I'm so sorry I can't get up just yet."

"No, ma'am. I'm sorry to be bothering you. I didn't know…"

"Sit right down here. You must be Jack, and this must be Alice." She reached out her hands. Replacement went right over and sat next to her. Jack sat down in a high-back chair and Thomas sat in a chair next to his wife.

"Can I get you anything? I just put a pie in the oven, but would you like something to eat?"

"No, thank you, sir. I only have a few questions."

"You take your time, son." Thomas reached out and squeezed his wife's hands. "We go to church with your grandmother. If there's anything, anything at all, we can do…"

His wife patted his leg. "My Thomas has a caring heart. We knew your father, Jack. He was a lovely boy."

"Thank you, ma'am. You were the police dispatcher?"

"I was the dispatcher for everything. Police, fire, and the EMTs. Among other things—secretary, log keeper, bottle washer." She smiled.

"Did you take the emergency call that night?"

She nodded. "It was a young girl. She was just about hysterical. I couldn't make everything out, but I called Henry and the fire station to send the ambulance. The systems weren't connected then."

"Did you get a call before that one? One about a fight or any disturbance at Buckmaster Pond?"

"No. It was a real quiet day and an even quieter night."

"I read the report about the call. Henry Cooper was on Cushing Street?"

"Yes, Henry was on patrol that night." She nodded and sat up straighter.

"What kind of man is Henry?" Jack's question caused Gracie to frown.

"Henry is a troubled soul. I hope and pray for him, but he's always battled his own demons: drink, women, anger. He has a lot of flaws; we all do."

"So, Henry was on patrol but Frank Nelson came out to Buckmaster too?"

"Of course. Frank takes his job very seriously. He said he sleeps with the police scanner next to his bed."

"Do you know Frank well?"

"He's a fine man." Gracie smiled. "I've known him for almost thirty-five years. We worked together for twenty. He's dedicated his life to community service. I think that's why he never married."

"Does he live alone?"

"He's got a place over on Forester Ave." Thomas pointed north.

"Did Frank take a cruiser home with him?"

"Yes. We had three cruisers at that time. They usually left one at the station but Henry and Frank took theirs home."

Replacement leaned forward. "Was the third police car at the station that night?"

"No." Gracie shook her head.

Jack and Replacement exchanged a glance. "Where was that car?" Jack held his breath while he waited for her answer.

"We had it," Thomas said. "The chief and I went to Pinkerton for a conference."

"Are you sure? Why would you take a cruiser?"

"Sure I'm sure." Thomas nodded emphatically. "I was on the auxiliary force then. The chief was giving a talk to the volunteers in Pinkerton and ask me to come with him."

"Are you positive it was that night?"

"One hundred and ten percent. Gracie got a hold of me and I told the chief. He drove back here like a bat outta hell. I've never been in a car going that fast. That man loved your father."

Gracie reached out and squeezed Thomas's hand. "Thomas did too. Steven was in his scout troop."

Thomas snapped his fingers and got up. "I've got something for you, Jack." He hurried out of the room.

"You were also the dispatcher for the fire department and EMTs?" Jack asked.

Gracie nodded.

"There's a little auxiliary fire station out near Buckmaster. Was it manned that night?"

"Oh, no. They just kept a truck out there. Back then, emergency services were all volunteers."

"Would you happen to know if I could get a list of who the volunteers were?"

Gracie sighed. "I can write one up for you. It may take a couple of hours and I'd like to call around." She tapped the side of her head. "The old brain power plant's not what it used to be."

Jack nodded.

Thomas came back in carrying a wooden plaque. "I'd like you to have this." He handed the plaque out to Jack.

The wooden board was stained a dark brown. Glued on the left side of the board was a compass. But mounted to the right was an engraved jackknife. In the middle of the board was a picture of a scout troop. "I'm not in the picture," Thomas said.

"He was taking the photograph," Gracie added proudly.

Thomas pointed to Steven in the front row. Standing behind him was the chief, Frank Nelson, Henry Cooper, and another young man.

Thomas said something else but Jack didn't hear him. He wasn't paying attention anymore. His eyes were focused on the photograph.

"Who's the young scout leader on the left?" Jack asked.

Thomas adjusted his glasses and looked over Jack's shoulder. "Oh, that's Kristine's brother, Dale."

"He's an EMT," Gracie added.

Jack held the board with both hands. "Thank you for this. It's very important to me."

CHAPTER 34

Jacked Up

Jack and Replacement walked into the garage. Jack frowned as he looked at the Impala on the lift; the gas tank was off.

Marty and Matty stood underneath it, working. Marty saw them come in and walked over.

"How's my car?"

"It's jacked up. It was sugar in the gas tank. Good news is whoever did it really hates you. They used too much sugar. It gunked up the gas lines before too much got to the engine. I don't think it damaged the engine, but we have to flush everything out and I should replace the lines." Marty wiped his hands on a greasy rag.

"How long?"

Marty rubbed the back of his neck. "We have to take off the tank, flush everything, replace the lines…at least a couple days."

Jack didn't want to ask the next question. "How much?"

"It ain't gonna be cheap." Marty looked back at the car. "The engine's got a lot of miles on her. You might want to think about—"

"Nope. Fix her."

Marty nodded.

"Officer Stratton?" Matty called out to Jack as Matty stood under the Impala.

The tone of his voice was enough to give Jack pause, but when Jack saw the look on Matty's face, he knew something was wrong.

"I think you should see this." Matty waved him over.

Everyone followed Jack over to the Impala. Matty was short enough to stand under the car when it was on the lift, but Jack had to duck.

"Look at this." Matty pointed to a spot inside the back bumper.

Jack moved closer and noticed the small black box.

"Is this some kind of hide-a-key?" Matty asked. "I went to take it off," Matty grabbed it. "But the magnet is really strong."

"Don't." Jack's voice was low and commanding.

Matty's hand froze.

"I'm an officer in Darrington, and we all have GPS on our off-duty cars." Jack forced a smile and patted Matty on his back as he lied. "Nice job, though."

"That sucks. They track you off duty, too?" Matty rolled his eyes.

Jack looked at Replacement. Her green eyes were at a low burn.

"Well, thank you for your time. Let me know when it's done."

Jack and Replacement walked across the lot to the little blue Bug.

"Do you want to drive?" Jack held up the keys.

She took the keys but didn't say anything.

When Jack got right next to the back of the car, he squatted down as if he was tying his shoe. He reached under the bumper until he felt a square box.

Someone else has been following me too.

Jack stood up and got in the passenger seat. He had to put his seat almost all the way back to fit in.

"You okay?" she asked with the smile stuck on her face.

"Yeah."

"Where to?"

"Ron's Bait, Tackle, and Sports."

Replacement pulled out and headed north. Traffic was light so she could relax behind the wheel. After a few miles, her light drumming on the steering wheel turned into more aggressive strikes.

"Someone put a GPS on your car?" She kept looking straight ahead.

"They put one on this car too."

"What?" Replacement looked down as if she were now sitting on a bomb.

"It's actually a good thing."

"A good thing?" Her voice went high. "I don't see how that can be a good thing."

"I'm going to use it."

"Is that why we're going to Ron's?"

"That's part of it."

"Is the person following us now?"

"I hope so. I want them to know I went to Ron's."

"What're we getting there?" Replacement asked.

"I have a list."

Fifteen minutes later, Jack handed his list across the counter to Ron.

Ron adjusted his glasses as he read down the list of equipment that Jack needed. "I've got everything except the dry suit."

Jack clicked his tongue.

"You could try Finneran's Scuba in Yardborough. It's about four hours up north." Ron glanced at his watch. "They'd be closed by the time you get there."

Jack shook his head. "I'm going at first light."

Replacement's mouth dropped open. "You're planning on going scuba diving? Where?"

"Buckmaster."

Her eyes widened. "You're going to look for it."

Jack nodded.

"Why do you need a dry suit? Can't you use a wet suit?"

"No. The water's too cold." Jack drummed his hands on the counter.

Ron leaned against the counter. "You could use a wet suit and just duct tape the wrists and openings. You can put some really warm water down the suit, and you should be good to go for twenty or twenty-five minutes. I wouldn't push it more than that."

"Twenty-five at a time?"

"Yeah, but make sure you warm up in between." Ron vigorously nodded his head. "You're risking hypothermia, a frozen regulator, or a host of bad things that you don't want to happen when you're underwater."

"What about the regulator? You have an ice regulator, right?"

Ron nodded. "I got one. Still, keep the dive to twenty-five minutes. Any more and you're asking for problems."

Jack grabbed a roll of duct tape and turned back to the clerk. "Great. I'll take the wet suit in petite."

Ron and Replacement both looked at him, confused.

"Alice," Jack lowered his voice and put his hand on her shoulder, "I didn't plan on going myself. I need you to go in for me."

Replacement shook as though someone hit her with a Taser. "Me?" she gasped. "I can't even swim."

"You just have to hold onto a rope while I lower you into the water."

"Lower me into the water? Freezing cold water? Are you crazy?"

Jack laughed.

She slammed both hands into his chest, and he laughed harder.

"You big jerk." She punched him in the arm.

"I'll take one men's wet suit made to fit a big jerk, please." Jack handed Ron his credit card.

CHAPTER 35

A Piece of Garbage

Thick, gray clouds swirled overhead. Even though the sun had risen, it was still dark and gloomy. Jack darted out of the back of the inn, carrying the duffel bag filled with his gear, to Kristine's car. With the GPS on the Bug, he had to leave it there. He didn't want to be followed this morning.

He tossed the bag into the backseat and jumped in. He cranked up the heat and zipped his jacket. He wanted to warm himself as much as possible before he got there. By the time he pulled into Buckmaster's gravel parking lot, he was sweating.

He grabbed the heavy bag of gear and jogged the short distance to the pond with the pack across his back. Jack climbed onto the rocks and laid everything out.

He picked up the seven-inch jackknife and tied one end of thick fishing line onto it. Hanging off the line was a weight suspended with a round eyelet. He tested the weight to make sure it would slide along the line.

Toss the knife out and use the weight to follow the line to where it lands. It should work.

Jack stood up and prepared to throw the knife as far as he could but stopped.

He killed Steven. He stabbed him multiple times. It was a rage killing. Was his hate satisfied?

Jack tossed the knife underhand as though he was throwing away a piece of garbage. The knife splashed into the water, and the fishing line continued to play out until it finally stopped.

Jack hurriedly stripped down to his underwear. He'd gotten his dive certification awhile ago, but he was not that experienced. He forced himself to dress quickly. Once he was done, he taped all of the seams of the suit. He couldn't tell about the hood seam, but it would have to do.

He poured the two thermoses of hot water inside and grabbed his tank and mask. As he sat on the edge of the rock, he checked his regulator, compass, light, and the small metal detector in his left hand.

Jack bowed his head. "God, please," he whispered, and then slid into the water.

Not bad. Crystal-clear.

He followed the line. The pond was deep, and the sides dropped completely off. The light filtered down, and he could see the silty bottom. This part of the pond was like a tall cup that ended in a round base. The knife he had tossed landed almost directly in the center of the pond. Jack was surprised how small it was. The faint ping from the metal detector would occasionally get louder, but Jack was sure from all the years of fishing he'd get lots of false leads. His search grid slowly began to expand outward and then he felt the cold water on his back.

Damn.

He checked his watch. Eleven minutes. He was on borrowed time now. He kept slowly moving and working the grid that he had laid out in his head. At the end of a line, he'd switch ninety degrees and keep moving forward.

Sixteen minutes. At this depth, his chest was now starting to hurt from the cold. Jack knew his motor skills would be slowing soon, but he pushed on, forcing himself to move carefully.

Twenty-two minutes. He was past the mark he had set for himself. His hands trembled, and his breathing was getting ragged.

You gotta go, Jack. One more pass.

The debate he'd been having with himself continued. He was nearing the edges of the deep section of the pond, but he was rushing now.

Damn.

He looked back. He skipped a section. As he checked his watch, he noticed his whole arm was vibrating. Twenty-five minutes.

BEEP.

He had just pushed off when he heard the loud ping. He frantically turned himself around. Dirt and silt blocked his vision where he'd stirred up the bottom.

Idiot!

He swept the metal detector around until the beep was solid once more. His hand closed around a long, solid object. The silt swirled and settled. As it vanished and his hand appeared, he knew he held the weapon used to murder his father.

Jack pushed off again and headed up for the rocks. His chest tightened, and he had to work to breathe. The water was brutally cold and, as he thought about it, the cold became so intense it almost felt as if he were being burned.

He scrambled onto the rocks and tore at his wet suit. With trembling fingers, he stripped naked and dried himself off. His clothes offered no warmth as his hands fumbled with the buttons and zippers.

He looked down at the rusted knife on the rock. It was a jackknife covered in rust. Even so, he could see that the tip had been broken off. A chill colder than the frigid water ran through him. He found it—*the jackknife!*

CHAPTER 36

Damaged Goods

Jack and Replacement stood in their room at the inn. On the table, in an evidence bag, was the jackknife.

"Now what?" Replacement asked.

Jack pointed at the evidence bag. "That's the bait. Now we need to wiggle the hook." He took out his phone.

"Who're you calling?" Replacement asked.

"Jeff Franklin."

"The reporter?" Replacement's hands went out.

Jack grinned.

Replacement moved next to Jack so she could listen.

"This is Jeff."

"Hi, Jeff. This is Jack Stratton. How'd you like a stop-the-presses exclusive?"

"Like a tick likes a dog!" Jeff blurted out.

Appropriate analogy, Replacement mouthed.

"I have one condition," Jack said. "This story has to be on the front page for tomorrow morning's paper."

Jack sat alone in his room at the inn, staring down at the jackknife in the evidence bag on the table. He found the weapon that murdered his father. Now he waited for the owner of the knife. He'd barely slept last night. He was up until after midnight, making phone calls and shoring up plans. Replacement insisted that he get a couple of hours of sleep and he finally laid down at two.

Footsteps in the hallway made him raise his head. There was a soft knock on the door.

Jack stood up, rolled his shoulder and cracked his neck.

Another knock was louder this time.

Jack strolled over and opened the door.

Lieutenant Frank Nelson was led into the room, followed by a uniformed state police trooper.

"You're wrong about this, Stratton," Nelson grumbled.

"No, I'm not." Jack held up the evidence bag. "Do you recognize this, Frank?"

Nelson stared at the knife for a moment. The muscles on the side of his head flexed as he chewed the inside of his mouth. "It's a scout knife."

The trooper behind him took a step forward.

"I lost mine years ago. Camping," Nelson quickly added.

Jack stepped back out of the doorway. "It's not yours. Everyone else is waiting in the other room."

The side door between the inn's rooms opened. In the room next door, Replacement, Kristine, Jimmy Tanaka, two more state troopers, and Officer Kenny waited. The trooper led Nelson into the room.

Replacement gave Jack a thumbs-up and Jack winked back.

Jack walked back over to the chair. Everything was now in place. Jack put the jackknife back on the table, sat down and crossed his arms.

The minutes ticked slowly by. The sky outside was just starting to lighten when there was another soft knock on the door.

Jack got up and answered the door.

Chief Dennis walked into the room. "Morning, Jack." He wasn't smiling. "Find anything?"

Jack pointed to the evidence bag on the table.

Dennis marched across the floor and glared down.

Jack shut the door. "I found the jackknife. The tip is busted off. I'm sure it will match."

"Nice work. The newspaper said you were sending it to the state lab for some type of new testing. Did you get anything else?"

"I uncovered witness testimony. Turns out that multiple witnesses saw emergency lights out at the pond the night my father was killed."

Dennis scoffed. "That ain't new, son. Police, ambulance—hell, even the fire department came out there that night."

"Yeah. But they didn't come out twice. Witnesses saw the police out there and then a half an hour later, they saw them again."

Dennis exhaled and looked down at his feet. "You got a name for this witness?"

Jack ignored the question. "There was nothing in the police report about a cruiser being anywhere near Buckmaster."

Dennis looked up at Jack, and his mouth slowly opened. "Do you think...Henry Cooper? He was the officer on duty. He knew Steven. Cooper's a drunk. He was Steven's scout leader. That's a scout knife, right? The leaders all got knives."

"Shut up, Dennis." Jack's voice was a low growl. "You need some acting lessons before you try that BS story."

Dennis's hands curled into fists. "Watch your mouth, boy."

"Save it. All the scouts got a jackknife. You did too. There were three police cruisers in town. Cooper was fifteen minutes away from the pond. He checked in regularly. Nelson was home. Your father was at a convention."

"You flunked math, I take it?" Dennis scoffed. "You just accounted for all the police cars. So tell me this, Sherlock. How'd these witnesses see police lights if none of the cruisers were there?"

"Because you drove Steven there."

"Your old man lived just down the street. Why would I drive him?"

"Because Steven suspected something was up. Terri invited him out to the pond. Steven asked his best friend to come along with him and watch his back. It's what I would have done. Your father was out of town, so you drove his personal car. The one with the bubble light that you're so proud of."

Dennis's face morphed into a deep scowl. "You think you have it all figured out?" he spat.

"Most of it."

Dennis looked over at Jack's holster on the table, and his hand went to rest on his gun. "Why don't you tell me all that you have then, smart guy? What's this new test?"

Jack shifted his weight.

Dennis drew his gun. "Don't even think of moving, kid. You're not that fast. Put your hands up. Get on your knees."

"Fine." Jack lowered himself to the floor and held his hands out and up. "I need to know something first."

"I thought you figured it all out?" Dennis sneered.

"Like I said, most of it."

"Ask away. It'll be our secret. Then I got a couple of questions for you."

"Steven went to talk to Terri while you waited in the parking lot. When Terri's brothers jumped him, you heard the fight. You grabbed your father's bubble light, turned the siren on and scared them off. I figured that part out but—"

"But you don't know why?" Dennis sneered.

"Noooo." Jack dragged the word out as if he were pulling taffy. He let the cocky grin spread broadly across his lips as he did. "I figured out the why too. That part was easy once I was sure it was you."

"Really, smart guy? Why do you think I did it?"

"See, it's explaining the why to you that could be a problem for me. I know I'm right but, if I tell you, you're going to get so mad that you might even kill me right away. I need you to promise to wait until I'm completely finished." Jack flashed a big smile.

"You arrogant little snot. Fine. Let me hear the whys."

Jack settled back on his legs and cracked his neck. "You loved Patty."

Dennis's eyes widened before he scoffed. "What? You're way off, kid. I've been with the same gal since junior high."

"Yeah, I know all about your wife. Mayor's kid marrying the police chief's kid? That's right out of a storybook, except you loved Patty. I found the valentine that you gave her. I thought it was nothing because you wrote DJ. I thought the *J* stood for someone's last name but that's what they called you when you were little, right? DJ is short for Dennis *Junior.*"

"What valentine?"

"The one you gave Patty. It had three arrows in it. That's a lot of love."

The corner of Dennis's mouth turned up. "I gave Patty a valentine. So what?"

"You loved Patty, but her scumbag father molested her. A police report was filed. That means that your father looked into it. Is that why you dumped her?"

"My mother told me what Patty's father did to her. I had to break up with Patty. My mother made me. Patty was damaged goods."

Jack fought down his snarl. "So you drove Steven to Buckmaster Pond that night, and you waited in the car. You heard the fight. You turned the bubble light on and everyone ran away. Then you come up. Steven's lying there, beaten, but he told you. Steven told you that Patty, the girl you love, is pregnant but it's with his kid, and that hate just went right through you. You thought about how the girl you love is going to have Steven's child. She loved Steven. Everyone loved Steven more than you. Even your father—"

"Screw you." Spit flew from his mouth. "You don't know crap. Everyone talks about my old man like he was some great guy, but they shouldn't. He wasn't. I was his son. Me. But it was always Steven. Steven did this. Steven did that. Never me. I always had to bring Steven along whenever we did anything and then—"

Jack tried to relax his legs. "Then what?"

"Steven shouldn't have gone near Patty."

"You have to be kidding, right? Did Steven even know you loved Patty? Did you ever tell him?"

"How could I? My mother…"

"So Steven didn't even know. He never saw it coming, did he?"

Dennis shook his head.

"You're such a pansy."

Dennis raised the gun. "Tell me everything you got, and I'll make it fast," Dennis said.

"I haven't asked all my questions yet. You killed Steven—"

"Who are the new witnesses?"

"That comes at the end." Jack smirked. "I'm not done. Your father was looking into the murder. He figured it out, too."

"I thought I got away with it but my father wouldn't let it go." Dennis took a step forward. "Then one day he comes home and…I just knew. I knew he'd figured it out that it was me."

"How did you kill him?"

Dennis leaned in and grinned as if he were sharing a fishing tip. "He had a bad heart. Everyone was telling him to take a vacation, but no, he wouldn't stop. He kept digging for who killed his precious little Steven. He used to call Steven his 'other son.' Other son? I'm his son. His *only* son. But night and day, that's all he talked about. Steven. I always knew he liked Steven more than me but now everyone in town knew it too. He mourned for him like someone killed his real son. I just wanted him dead too. I tried switching his heart medicine. The old fool didn't see that, either, but it didn't kill him."

"So you didn't have the guts—"

"Shut up, boy. One night, he came home and I knew he'd figured it out. He looked broken. He came upstairs so we could talk. He started crying. But I knew he wasn't crying for me. He was going to take me in. ME! Arrest his *real* son. So, at the top of the stairs…I gave him a little push."

Keep talking, you fat idiot.

"I hoped he'd break his neck. It was a bonus he had a heart attack. He just lay there, begging. I waited until he finally shut up and his eyes went gray; then I knew I was free."

"Until I showed up." Jack winked and clicked his tongue. "It was you who took the shot at me at the pond."

"But you were too stupid to leave. I just wanted you gone. I wouldn't have had to kill you if you had enough sense to just go. Why didn't you leave? I didn't want it this way. You're Patty's son. I tried to scare you off."

"Do you know why I didn't go? I didn't go anywhere so I could avenge my father's murder. You butchered him, so there was no way I was letting you get away with it."

"You're not avenging anything, boy. They'll look for your killer, but they'll never find him. I'll make it look good. Just like I did all these years. I'll pull out all the stops. I'll call in everyone. Hell, I'll even set my son up to console that pretty little pet who follows you around. I'll make sure that he takes good care of her."

Jack's cold stare made Dennis shut up. "Here's the last part, Dennis. This is what you've been waiting for." Jack savored the moment and let the silence build. "You're under arrest."

Both doors to the hotel room burst open.

"FREEZE!" Four voices bellowed the command as the state troopers leveled their guns at Dennis.

Dennis looked around, bewildered. His shoulders slumped and he threw his gun onto the bed. He looked at Jack in disbelief. "Why didn't you just leave?"

Jack scoffed. "How the hell can I explain it to you? My whole life I wanted to know who my father was, and you killed yours. You wouldn't get it."

The state police captain nodded to Nelson.

Nelson motioned to Kenny. "Cuff him, Kenny," Nelson ordered.

Kenny hesitantly walked around the state police officers and over to his former boss.

"You're still crazy, Stratton." Tank grinned broadly.

"Thanks for the assist. Did you hear everything?"

Tank nodded. "Every word."

"Good work, everyone," the captain said. "Martinez and I will take him to Rosemont. Billings and Tank will stay to pack up."

Kristine slipped into the room and held up a slender hand. "Can you *please* be careful when you move the armoire back? It's delicate." She gave the captain a smile fraught with worry.

Kenny frowned as he took out his handcuffs. "Hands behind your back, Chief."

Jack watched Kenny. He could almost hear his police academy instructor's voice yelling at Kenny for poor procedure. "Your feet are too close together. You need to grab the suspect's other wrist to control him."

Jack started to say something but his warning came too late.

Dennis yanked Kenny's arm and pivoted around him. Dennis ripped Kenny's gun from its holster.

Kenny stumbled forward.

Dennis grabbed Kristine and pulled her in front of him.

Jack's gun snapped up, but there was no clear shot.

Kristine winced and then froze as Dennis pressed the muzzle of the gun against her head.

No one moved.

"Throw your guns on the bed now." Spit flew from Dennis's mouth as he tried to shield his body with Kristine's.

"Not going to happen." Jack aimed down the sight.

"Now!" Dennis shrieked. "I'll blow her head off! I'll do it! I will!"

Damn. He's lost it.

The captain held out a hand. "Dennis, calm—"

"Toss them—NOW," Dennis ordered.

The captain tossed his gun on the bed and the rest of the officers, including Jack, followed suit.

Dennis's hand shook. "I need time. A head start. I deserve a head start. I'll let her go when I get out of town."

Kristine was crying. Tears ran down her face.

"All of you get against the wall. Hands behind your heads." Dennis leveled the gun at Jack. "Not you. Hands up."

Jack raised his hands higher.

The gun in Dennis's hand shook as he pointed it at Jack's face. "It's all your fault. Everything is. If you just left the dead buried…DAMN YOU."

Kristine looked at Jack and her expression changed. Jack could see the resolve in her eyes. Her chin trembled but her lips pressed together into a determined line. "Damn you, Dennis." Her voice cracked. "Steven was your best friend."

"It was his fault!" Dennis yelled.

"No…it was mine," Kristine whispered.

"No, it wasn't." Jack shook his head.

"I won't let you hurt his son." Kristine closed her eyes.

Jack could see Kristine's body tighten up as she prepared to move.

Dennis must have felt the change in the body he was using as a human shield. He pressed the gun back against her head.

He sees it coming…

Kristine's eyes snapped open. She stopped crying. "I'm so sorry, Jack." Her voice was strangely calm.

"Dennis, look at your chest." Jack's order was crisp and direct.

Dennis glanced down and looked back up, puzzled. A red laser dot was centered on the middle of his white shirt.

"On the other end of that dot is a fifty-caliber sniper rifle with the best marksman I know dying to pull the trigger. I lower my hands, you die. I close my fist, you die."

Dennis's face went as white as his shirt, and he squinted as he tried to look through the darkened doorway at the sniper in the next room.

The laser dot shifted to his face. Blinded, he winced and turned his head away. Dennis glared at Jack but the gun trembled in his hands. He aimed the gun at Jack's head. "We've got a standoff then. I'll blow your head off. We'll both die."

"You won't shoot."

"Why?"

"You ever see what a fifty-caliber round does to someone?" Dennis went even whiter. "That, and the fact that you're a coward, means you won't shoot me. Throw your gun down."

Dennis gripped the gun tighter. "Coward? You want to die, boy? Do you?"

Jack stepped forward. "You know what? I do. Ever since I can remember, I wanted to die so I could get out of the hell I found myself in. And that feeling hasn't stopped. It's only gotten worse. Every day, I have to come up with reasons not to eat a bullet. It's wrong that I don't value my life more, but you value yours way too much. You could shoot me, and I might die. But you suck as a shot, so I may not. Even at this range. But that doesn't matter because live or die, I don't care! You? They won't miss. You'll die, and you don't want to. Throw the gun down now or I close my hand."

"You rotten bastard."

"You made me a bastard!" Jack screamed. "I had a chance…" His hand shook. "Five. Four."

Dennis's face contorted in rage. "I'm just sorry that I didn't kill Steven before he slept with Patty." Dennis's eyes shifted to the doorway and the unseen sniper.

Jack stopped breathing. He knew there was no sniper in the other room. It was Alice with his dad's laser pointer.

Dennis pivoted. He aimed for the red dot in the doorway.

Jack pushed forward off the balls of his feet.

The gun discharged. In the small room, the blast sounded like a cannon. The laser dot blinked out.

Jack's left hand caught the chief's right wrist and shoved it up. The gun fired again. Jack twisted Dennis's wrist and Dennis screamed in pain.

Every police officer in the room turned and tackled Dennis to the floor.

Jack ripped the gun from Dennis's hand.

"ALICE!" Jack charged into the other room.

Replacement laid sprawled on her stomach on the floor. Her back was to him and she wasn't moving.

Jack rushed over and turned her on her side. Jack's army training took over. His hands searched for a wound while he covered her with his own body. "Status?" Jack yelled.

Replacement blinked rapidly and just stared at him.

"Status?" Jack bellowed again as his hands continued to sweep over her body.

"What does that mean?" Replacement barked back. "Am I okay? Yeah."

Jack pulled her close and held her.

Replacement started to shake.

"It's okay." Jack whispered.

"Okay?" Replacement struggled to pull free. "It's totally okay." She jumped up. "You were awesome." Her face lit up with a grin from ear to ear. "I was so scared when he grabbed Kristine and then pointed the gun at you." She held up the laser pointer. "I was going to try running out to the hallway and stabbing him with the pen part when he came out of the room but then I had the whole laser sight idea."

Jack's head ticked to the side. "I'm really glad you went with plan B."

"Yeah." She grinned. "Me too. He totally fell for it."

Jack put his arm around her shoulder and they walked back to the doorway. Their hotel room was trashed. The captain had finished handcuffing Dennis, who sat on the floor. The corner desk had been knocked over and paper littered the ground.

Dennis groaned as he straightened his legs out.

"Don't move," Nelson ordered.

"Shut up, you putz," Dennis snapped. "I'm not going anywhere…" Dennis's voice trailed off.

Jack followed his eyes. Dennis stared at the floor. In the middle of the scattered pile of papers, an old red valentine stuck out.

"Patty kept the valentine," Dennis said softly. "Jack?"

"What?"

"Will you tell Patty something for me? Tell her I love her. I always have. I just couldn't…"

The state police captain pointed; two troopers walked over to Dennis and pulled him to his feet.

Jack stared into the eyes of the man who killed his father. Part of him wanted to draw his gun and finish his quest for vengeance then and there. He knew no one could stop him. He was too fast. Draw, safety, pull the trigger—over. Less than a fraction of a second.

Jack could almost feel the gun kicking back in his hand. He could see Dennis crumpling to the ground as he unloaded the clip into him. But he also saw the look on Alice's face. The sadness. The disappointment. The pain.

What would happen to her?

Jack felt Replacement's hand slide into his.

"You're not worth killing." Jack let the words fall from his mouth.

Dennis hung his head and let the troopers lead him out of the room.

CHAPTER 37

Miss Ultra-Hypocritical

Jack tossed another bag in the Impala and headed back to the inn. The sky was a brilliant blue, and the air was crisp but not too cold. He wanted to break into a run and feel the air on his face as he walked along the gravel path.

Jack broke into a run. He couldn't wait to see Replacement's face. As he pushed through the door, three women turned around. Kristine had her arm around Jack's grandmother, and Replacement stood next to the old woman and held her hand.

"Jackie." Mrs. Ritter smiled and held out her arms.

Jack went over, and she embraced him once more.

"You promise?" She patted his cheek and rubbed his back.

"Yes. I'll be sure to visit. Let me get things settled, and I'll be back. It's not that far."

"I'll make sure he calls," Replacement offered as she rose up on her toes. She had on her pink "I Love Hope Falls" shirt with matching baseball hat.

"When you come, you'll always have a room here." Kristine hugged her.

"Oh, nonsense." Mrs. Ritter huffed. "Next visit, they stay with me."

They laughed and exchanged another round of hugs. Kristine kissed Jack's left cheek and Mrs. Ritter his right. Loaded down with homemade sandwiches and drinks, they waved and walked out to the parking lot.

"I'm really going to miss it here." Replacement kicked the ground before she twirled around. "I watched the sunrise from the widow's walk this morning after you left. I don't think I've ever seen one so pretty. Where did you go?"

"I had to get a few things. I want to make a pit stop on the way home," Jack advised her.

"Where? Crud."

Jack followed her eyes to the parking lot.

"What?" He shrugged.

"Look." She pouted and pointed.

Jack looked again. There were only three cars parked there: his Impala, a green sedan, and the blue Beetle.

"What's wrong?"

"Someone rented my car." She scooted over to the Beetle and gave it a hug.

"Wait a second, Miss Ultra-Hypocritical. You give me a hard time about the Impala, but you get to hug your car?"

"This is different." She stood and pouted. "It's so cute." She stood straight up. "What do you mean *your* car?"

Jack tossed a set of keys to her and smiled. "I'll follow you so you don't get lost."

Replacement caught the keys but just stood there, staring.

Jack shrugged as he went to get into the Impala.

Replacement stared down at the keys as she tapped her foot. "What is this?"

Jack smiled.

"What do you mean? Are you serious? You didn't? You did? You bought me the car?"

"I saw the sign at the rental place that it was for sale. It's pretty used and the guy gave me a good price on it."

Replacement's mouth hung open. "How can I repay you?"

"Forget it."

"Mine? I never had my own car. Ah!"

She raced over to the Impala. She frantically hugged Jack's head through the window and rocked him back and forth.

"Replacement, let me go."

She danced over to hug her new used car. She laughed and wiped her eyes as she jumped behind the wheel. "Where are we going?"

"I need to go see someone before we go home."

CHAPTER 38

What's My Name?

Jack carried the small box over and set it down on the table. Patty rocked back and forth and looked down at her hands. The doctor stood in the corner of the room, with Replacement next to him.

"Hi." Jack smiled as he sat down.

Patty gave him a quick wave, and her eyes darted to his face and then away.

"I wanted to stop by and see you again."

"Patty, this is Jack. We talked about him this morning." The doctor nodded his head and smiled.

Patty looked over, and she let her eyes stop on Replacement. Patty squinted as she stared at Replacement's pink shirt. A little smile slowly dawned on her face. "Hope Falls," Patty whispered.

Jack nodded and leaned closer. "We were just there. You grew up there."

Patty nodded and scooted forward in her chair. She leaned closer and turned her head so the doctor couldn't see what she said. "Steven...why did he call you Jack?"

Damn. This is going to be hard to explain.

Jack shrugged and opened the box. "I picked up a couple things for you. I have some more, but they said you can only have two for right now."

Jack reached in and pulled out a stuffed animal. It was a dog, and it was missing an ear.

"Alphie?" Patty rose partway out of her chair, and her hand hovered over the toy. "It's my Alphie!" She looked up at Jack, and he nodded.

"It's yours."

She snatched it to her chest and buried her face against it. Jack watched her as she rocked back and forth, cradling it. After a few minutes, he heard the doctor step forward, but he held up a hand.

Give her some time.

Jack watched and waited. After a few more minutes, she looked up and her eyes darted to Jack and then to the box and back down like a little kid. Jack reached inside and took out the picture frame. Patty's mouth fell open before he even turned it over. Her hand flashed out and stopped as it touched his. Jack looked at her, but her eyes darted away, and she pulled her hand back.

He set the picture frame down on the table and turned it around.

Patty inhaled and sat up straighter. She leaned down close and smiled. "Momma."

Jack nodded.

"Momma and me."

Jack looked up to the ceiling and then put his hands on the table and shut his eyes. He felt her hand cover his. Slowly, he opened his eyes; something deep within them seemed to change.

She laid her arm flat on the table, rested her head on her arm and stared at him. "I'm sorry I wasn't a better mother to you."

Her words were so clear and sharp they slammed into him.

"What?" His voice broke.

"I'm sorry I sucked at being a mother. Dragging you all over. Everything."

He didn't know what to say. "It's okay."

Tears rolled down her cheeks.

Jack swallowed. "What's my name?"

She wrinkled her nose. "Steven. Like your father."

Replacement softly gasped.

His mother stroked the back of his hand, as he sat there, stunned.

"Steven?" She whispered the word.

"Yes?"

She held his hand. "Stev…" She made a face and looked away. "Sorry. It's just…hard for me."

"What's hard?" Jack asked.

"To say your name." Patty touched her heart. "It hurts. Besides Momma, Steven was the only person ever nice to me." She sniffled. "I guess that's why I don't say it much. I miss him."

Jack squeezed her hand. "He loved you too, Mom."

She smiled. "Thank you for bringing these." She held up Alphie.

"Sure." Jack nodded. "Next time I'll bring you some more stuff."

CHAPTER 39

I Had A Book

Jack lay in bed and stared up at the ceiling. His eyes followed along the cracks, and he put his arms out to either side. They would be moving tomorrow down to the two-bedroom apartment below them.

He exhaled and sighed. His eyes had just closed when he heard the faint tap at the bedroom door. It slowly opened, and Replacement's face appeared, her green eyes shining.

"You asleep?" she whispered.

"Yes."

She snorted and walked in, dragging her comforter and carrying her pillow.

Jack sat up.

"Do you want me to sleep on the couch? Do you want the bed?" He started to get up but stopped when she shook her head.

"I want the bed, but I don't want you to sleep on the couch." She looked up nervously.

Jack raised an eyebrow.

"We can still do the pillow thing down the middle." Her shoulders popped up and down. "I just don't want to sleep alone."

Jack nodded. He moved over, and she scooted up next to him.

"Thanks." She fanned the comforter out and wiggled around until she was comfortable. "You couldn't sleep?"

Jack shook his head. "I was thinking."

"About what?"

"My parents. In Florida. I haven't seen them in a while, so I'm going to go down and visit them."

"When?"

"Next month maybe. I have the time at work."

They both lay there and gazed up at the ceiling. Jack continued to follow the cracks until they faded off into the darkness.

"Would you have believed that?"

"What?" Replacement rolled onto her elbow to look at Jack.

He closed his eyes for a second before he continued. "Patty. She said my name is Steven."

Replacement nodded, and her hand ran softly over his.

"I'm going to change my name." Jack closed his eyes.

Replacement sat up. "You're not going to be Jack anymore?"

"No." Jack shook his head. "I'll still be Jack. That's like...who I am. It would be too weird to change that."

"Good. I like Jack."

"I was thinking…I'm going to change it to Jack Alton Steven Stratton."
He turned and looked at her. She smiled at first but then made a face.
"What?"
Replacement rolled onto her back and pressed her lips together.
"What? You don't like the sound of that?" Jack's voice rose.
"I like it. I really do. I think that's very nice of you, but…" She held her hands up. "Could you go with Jack Steven Alton Stratton?"
Jack shrugged. "Why?"
"Well, if you go with it the other way…you'll be Jack A.S.S." She burst out with a laugh.
Jack's mouth fell open, and then closed with a pop. He rolled on his back and burst out laughing, too. They both lay there until their laughter faded into the occasional snicker and, finally, contented sighs.
Jack closed his eyes, and he could feel sleep slowly clouding his thoughts.
Replacement rolled over. "How long are you going to be gone?"
"I was thinking a week with my folks. They live right outside Orlando."
Replacement shrugged.
"Would you want—would you want to go with me?"
Her face scrunched up.
"There's not much to do there; it's a retirement community. Pretty low-key, but they're not too far from Disney World. We could go to the park—"
His words were choked off, along with his air supply, as Replacement rolled on top of him. With her legs straddling his stomach, she sat up and raised her hands over her head and cheered. "Woo-hoo. I always wanted to go. Always!" She drummed her hands on his chest.
"That's sorta why I'm asking." Jack grinned.
"I know all about it. I had a book. It's not just one park. There are different ones. It's really cool."
Jack nodded.
"Let me tell you about them…"
Jack slowly drifted off to sleep as Replacement ran down her ever-lengthening list of the things they'd do together in the Magic Kingdom.

CHAPTER 40

It's Me

Jack relaxed into the front seat of the Impala and smiled. He felt great. For the past three days, all he'd done was sleep; the nightmares had stopped. Replacement shut off his alarm, so he slept until almost noon.

This morning was different: not bad, just different. His eyes had flashed open, and he just seemed to know what he had to do. It was as though he made a checklist while he was sleeping, and he hurried out of bed to get started on it.

The Impala turned onto the road to Hope Falls. Jack had written a hasty note for Replacement and slipped away. It was a long drive, but with no traffic, he made great time. It was still early, and everything was quiet in the little town.

The first stop was the library. One lone interior light was on inside, but he knew it was closed. He sighed as he walked up to the entrance and looked in. He could almost feel the calmness and smell the wood.

Maybe I'll stop back after I see my grandmother.

Jack grinned. He was looking forward to his surprise visit. He'd decided to come only this morning, so he hadn't called, but he was sure she wouldn't mind.

That's the third stop. First here.

Jack turned and opened the book return chute. He looked down to the wrapped package in his hands and smiled. Inside were the two yearbooks and an apology card from Replacement for "accidentally" borrowing them. She'd found them when they were unpacking and wanted to drive back right then. He told her he'd take care of it.

As he slid the package inside and closed the door, he suppressed the urge to pick up the phone and thank her. Before she wrapped the yearbooks, he'd taken another look at his parents' photos. Replacement hadn't said anything to him, but when he looked at Patty's photo, the graffiti someone had written about her was gone. The paper was only a little more frayed now, but you couldn't tell that someone had defaced it.

She didn't say anything. She's good like that.

Jack ran his hand through his hair and headed back to the car. The Impala restarted with a deep roar and Jack smiled and patted the dashboard. She'd been running even better since Atlas Auto had flushed her out. He slipped her into drive and headed back down the road.

He pulled onto the main road and hit the gas. The Impala purred, and he settled back into the seat to enjoy the feeling as the car softly rose and fell as the speed increased. His fingers gripped the wheel lightly, and he listened to the engine hum.

Is this content or happy? Maybe it's both?

Jack looked down at his chest and grinned as he inhaled. He pulled the rearview mirror down and a man who needed a shave with deep-brown eyes stared back. Jack smiled and flipped the mirror up.

He lowered his head and was about to push the pedal to the floor when he saw the sign up ahead. He let the car slow way down before he pulled in. His head swiveled around in a full scan, but he knew he was alone.

The Hope Falls Cemetery was set on a few acres of carefully maintained ground. It was an older cemetery and large trees ringed the edges. In the middle, a huge oak rose up, its thick branches spread out.

Jack's jaw clenched, and he could feel his muscles tighten as a somberness seeped in. He looked from the small headstones to a statue of a weeping angel draped over a tomb, its wings hanging in perpetual sorrow. He turned his head away as the sight of a lone teddy bear against a grave crashed into his chest.

Jack tried to only look forward as he headed for the back left corner. He never did well with death and in his twenty-six years had seen more than most. A gallery of faces flashed at the edges of his thoughts.

None of us make it out of here alive.

As he reached the back, he stopped and shut the car off. He was grateful that Kristine had told him right where it was so he didn't have to search. He walked slowly down a slightly worn path he was certain must have been made by Kristine and his grandmother on their trips to the little headstone.

His father was buried beside his grandfather. On the granite marker were the words: BELOVED SON. STEVEN RITTER.

Two weeks ago, I didn't even know him. Now...

Jack hung his head and stood there silently for a moment. The first breeze of the morning stirred the grass, and Jack looked up.

"Hi, Dad. It's me, Steven..."

EPILOGUE

Gathering Darkness

Marisa peered out into the gathering darkness. As still as the mannequin beside her, she peeked out of the window of her tattoo parlor at the large silver sedan parked across the street; its dark-tinted windows hid the occupants.

Like a little girl at the edge of the cellar stairs, she looked into the dark and the urge to turn and run washed over her. She didn't know why but she had the feeling someone was watching her.

What if they find me... I can't go back to that living hell again.

Marisa tried to shake all the old terrifying, paranoid thoughts from her head. She reached up and turned off the neon OPEN sign. Seemingly connected to the same switch, the sedan's headlights snapped on. A split-second later, it pulled away from the curb. She watched intently as the taillights of the sedan disappeared down the road.

"Marisa?" Joey called to her from behind the counter, breaking her from her trance.

Marisa didn't turn around as she locked the front door. She closed her eyes and tried to drive the old fears away. No one knows who she really is, she reminded herself. Still, even after all these years, she couldn't stop looking over her shoulder.

Joey nervously thrust his large tattooed arms deep into his pockets. "Ah...Marisa?" He looked more like an awkward teen than the tough guy he usually pretended to be. "Is there any chance that I could have tomorrow night off?"

"That's three days this week." Marisa raised an eyebrow as she walked over to the register.

"I know. But I need it and Shawn can't cover. It's kinda important."

"Just kinda?" Hiding a smile, Marisa didn't look up as she cashed out the register. She knew she'd cover for him but she wasn't going to say yes right away. She had a reputation as a hard-nosed business woman that she needed to perpetuate.

"No, it's big." Joey leaned against the counter and that goofy I'm-in-love smile that had been appearing regularly on his face showed up again. "I'm having dinner at Rosalie's." His eyes opened wide, "With her parents. First time," he added.

Marisa's face remained neutral as she continued to cash out. She was happy for him. Those little rituals make up a normal life. As she snapped a bill wrapper around the twenties in the drawer, she stared at the money.

Somewhere deep inside her chest, the empty ache hurt a little more. How she would have liked a little normal. To bring someone home to meet her parents...

"Marisa?" Joey's voice rose.

"Sure." Marisa nodded.

"Yes." Joey pumped his fist as if he made a game winning shot.

"I take it that things are going well with Rosalie?"

"Un-flippin'-believably good. She's... We talk about everything." Joey's head tipped to the side. "What about you?"

"Me?" Marisa walked over to the coffee machine and started to fill a thermos with some hot cocoa.

"Yeah. It's like a parade of guys keep coming in, tripping over their tongues to ask you out but you shoot them down right from the word 'go.'"

Marisa huffed and put a hand on her hip.

"You do." Joey pressed. "It's like a running joke. A guy comes in and asks you out and you're like 'NO.' Cutting him off like a guillotine."

"I do not."

"You do. Julie and I were cracking up guessing where the guy today would have taken you. I picked the symphony and she thought some wine tasting thing."

"The guy in the Audi?" Marisa laughed. "Since he couldn't take his eyes off my chest, I'd have a different guess about where he wanted to go."

"Not every guy is a creep..." Joey traced an invisible outline on the counter. "What about the cop?" He floated out the question without looking up. "That Jack guy."

When Marisa didn't answer, Joey slowly peeked up at her.

Marisa's lips were pressed in a firm line. Her brown eyes were as dark and cold as the night outside.

Joey stepped back from the counter and swallowed. "I, ah...I just... He seems like—"

She cut him off. "Let me know how your dinner goes." She opened the small refrigerator and took out a wrapped ham and cheese sandwich.

Joey sighed and headed for the door. "Sorry if I overstepped," he mumbled before he slipped out the back door.

As Marisa stood alone in the tattoo parlor that ache in her chest grew a little bigger again. *Jack.* The name hurt. It hurt to hear it. Thinking about him hurt even more.

Like a child, she hurried over to the closed door and stared hopefully out into the darkness, expecting him to walk around the corner at that instant. Jack had been assigned foot patrol downtown. She stood there looking out as a few snowflakes fell past the street light.

"Tu sei il bello mio," she whispered to the night. "You're my beautiful one."

She locked the door and turned the light out. Grabbing the thermos and sandwich, she headed out back. The heavy metal exit door closed with a loud bang.

The back alley was well lit and Marisa always made sure it stayed clean. Even the garbage bin and recycling container were neatly arranged. The space between the buildings was just wide enough to back a truck down, but tonight it was empty. Marisa started down the alley. Darkened rear doorways dotted the wall to the right.

As she approached, Marisa peered into each recess. She gingerly switched the sandwich to her right hand, careful not to squish it with the thermos.

The next alcove was covered in shadows. Out of the three lights above the little loading area, only one was still on. She hesitated. An errant snowflake landed on the back of her neck and she shivered.

Hurrying footsteps behind her made her jump. She turned on her heels.

A small, thin homeless man shuffled down the alley straight toward her. A thick, worn jacket flared out around him. Beneath the coat was a rainbow of different cloths and materials. The man slowed to a stop before her. His fingers twitched at his sides and his upper body rocked slightly back and forth. "Who's there?" The man ran his hand down his unkempt beard. Wild brown and gray hair poked out from underneath a brown knit cap pulled low. From underneath small round glasses, he gazed at Marisa with hungry eyes but his eyebrows pulled together warily.

"Hi, Thaddeus. It's me, Marisa." Marisa smiled and held out the sandwich and thermos.

"Oh." A broad smile crossed his face and his cheeks flushed red. "Evenin', Ms. Vitagliano." He eagerly reached out and took the gifts. "I really can't thank you enough."

"It's nothing." Marisa shrugged.

"It is to me." Thaddeus stepped back and looked at the ground.

"Are you sure you don't want to go to the shelter tonight? It's going to be cold."

Thaddeus shook his head and moved closer. Marisa tried not to wrinkle her nose at the smell. "I got layers." He pulled at his thick, worn jacket.

"If you get too cold, be sure to head over." Marisa smiled and walked past him.

"Will do, Ms. Vitagliano." He waved and then darted into a darkened doorway with his meal. "Thanks again," he called out.

Marisa wrapped her arms around her waist as she made her way back down the alley.

The whole stretch ahead was pitch black. She frowned. She just had the landlord fix that light. She made a mental note to take care of it tomorrow.

As she neared the darkness, she stopped. Snowflakes floated down around her face but something else drifted on the cold wind. The faintest whiff of cologne reached her nose. Bile rose up in her throat.

They say the strongest memories are not visual but scent. That smell resurrected a life that she thought she left buried in the past. Images slammed into her mind as she thought about that day she couldn't forget. The day everything good that she knew died. She shook. In her mind's eye, she could see his face once more.

"Hello, Angelica." A man in a H. Huntsman suit walked out of the shadows. "It's been a long time."

Her head trembled. She'd seen this killer's face in her dreams a thousand times but it had been years since she heard his voice. It cut deep. Old wounds ripped open and terror held her fast.

A malevolent grin spread across his face as he strode toward her. The heels of his expensive shoes on the tar sounded like gunshots to her ears. With each step, she flinched.

From some memory long since buried, she heard another voice that screamed to her from the past: "Run, Angelica! Run!"

She turned to flee but another man rushed out from the darkness and grabbed her. Her scream was cut off as a rag inside a large gloved hand clamped over her mouth. As she inhaled the fumes, the last thing she remembered was him...

Find out what happens next in the next thrilling installment: *Jacks Are Wild*

Handsome white knight Jack Stratton is back in this action-packed, thrilling adventure. When his sexy old flame disappears, no one thinks it's suspicious except Jack and one unbalanced witness. Jack feels in his gut that something is wrong. He knows that Marisa has a past, and if it ever caught up with her—it would be deadly.

Determined to buck the critics and listen to his instincts, he and his young feisty sidekick plunge ahead and start tracking down leads, hoping to find Marisa in time. The trail leads them into all sorts of trouble—landing them smack in the middle of an all-out mob war between the Italian Mafia and the Japanese Yakuza. When evidence surfaces that Marisa was kidnapped, Jack must navigate through the warring parties, assassins, and cold-blooded hit men to outwit the cunning kidnappers before it is too late. As the body count rises, the stakes in this game are life and death—with no rules except one: Jacks are Wild.

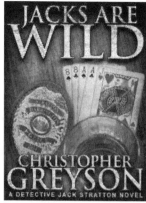

You could win a brand new
HD KINDLE FIRE TABLET
when you go to
ChristopherGreyson.com
and sign up for my newsletter.
No purchase necessary.
It's just my way of thanking my loyal readers.

Novels featuring Jack Stratton in order:
GIRL JACKED
JACK KNIFED
JACKS ARE WILD
JACK AND THE GIANT KILLER
DATA JACK
and coming soon… JACK OF HEARTS

Epic Fantasy
PURE OF HEART
Now Available

Looking for a mystery series mixed with romantic suspense?
Be sure to check out Katherine Greyson's bestselling series:
EVERYONE KEEPS SECRETS

Acknowledgments

I would like to thank all the wonderful readers out there. It's you who make the literary world what it is today—a place of dreams filled with tales of adventure. To all of you who have taken Jack and Replacement under your wings and spread the word via social media (Facebook Twitter) and who have spent the time to go back and write a great review, I say THANK YOU! Your efforts keep the characters alive and give me the encouragement and time to keep writing. I can't thank YOU enough.

Word of mouth is crucial for any author to succeed. If you enjoy the series, please consider letting others know or leaving a review at Amazon, even if it is only a line or two; it would make all the difference and I would appreciate it very much.

I would also like to thank my wife. She is the best wife, mother, and partner in crime that any man could have. My thanks also go out to my family, my fantastic editors: Faith Williams of The Atwater Group and Karen Lawson and Janet Hitchcock of The Proof is in the Reading, the unbelievably helpful Beta Readers, Kay Bloomberg, and my two awesome kids.

About the Author

Hello. Please allow me to introduce myself. My name is Christopher Greyson and I am a storyteller. Since I was a little boy, I dreamed of what mystery was around the next corner, or what quest lay over the next hill. If I couldn't find an adventure, one usually found me, and now I weave those tales into my stories. I am blessed to have written the bestselling Jack Stratton mystery series. The collection includes *Girl Jacked, Jack Knifed, Jacks Are Wild, Jack and the Giant Killer*, and *Data Jack*.

My background is an eclectic mix of degrees in theater, communications, and computer science. Currently I reside in Massachusetts with my lovely wife and two fantastic children. My wife, Katherine Greyson, who is my chief content editor, is an author of her own romance series, "Everyone Keeps Secrets."

I love to hear from my readers. Please go to ChristopherGreyson.com. In the next coming months, I plan to add free content including side stories and vignettes involving the characters from the series. Please sign up for my mailing list and receive periodic updates on this and new book releases. Thank you for reading my novels, and I hope my stories have brightened your day.

Sincerely,

Christopher Greyson

Alger

9:45 – Alger

9:00 – North First Floor
mam gram

Made in the USA
San Bernardino, CA
28 January 2016

S C